DEADLY START

CHARLOTTE DEAN MYSTERIES BOOK 1

PHILLIPA NEFRI CLARK

To Nas, Jade, Helen, my family and family-of-friends… this one is for you.
Mysteries abound

CHAPTER ONE

A LONG, LOW RUMBLE OF THUNDER WOKE CHARLOTTE DEAN. SHE pulled the sheet up to her chin, her sleepy eyes seeking the window beside the bed. For a moment, she'd thought she was in her room at Palmerston House, back in River's End where summer storms often swept in from the Great Southern Ocean. But the view here was over the main street of the small town she now called home.

Kingfisher Falls.

Despite the humid night, Charlotte shivered. She reached for the dressing gown on the end of the bed and threw it on as her toes fumbled around bare floorboards for slippers. Light flickered with the loud crash as thunder rolled again and the windows shook. She hurried out of the bedroom.

In the old kitchen, she filled the kettle. Tea was her go-to response during a storm, or any other stressful situation. The clock said it was almost four. Sleep time was over.

With her cup of tea warming her hands, Charlotte wandered around the house. Or was it an apartment? Whatever its designation, it sprawled over the top of the bookshop she'd moved here to work at. Three bedrooms, a large living room with a balcony over the street, two bathrooms—although one doubled as a laundry, and a small dining room through an archway. It was far too big for one person, but nobody had lived here in a long time and as Rosie Sibbritt, her new employer had insisted, it was time someone did.

How strange to live alone again after almost a year in a guest house with its revolving door of visitors.

She stared through the sliding door out to the balcony as rain began. The locals would rejoice. All she'd heard for the past few days was how dry the region was. Weeks ago, she'd visited Kingfisher Falls with Rosie's son, Trev, driving up from River's End for the day. Even then, the difference between the green coast of Victoria and inland landscape was noticeable, but now, with Christmas days away, long stretches of dry, hot weather had turned any sparse greenness to brown.

More thunder, and now, a flash of lightning forked into the trees at the top of the valley. Charlotte turned her back on the storm. After flicking on the one lamp in the place, she settled into an armchair with a book. Time to disappear into a world without storms and half-sad memories of her previous life.

The storm was replaced by sunshine by the time Charlotte ran down the stairs and unlocked the back door of the bookshop. One week in and she was opening the shop without Rosie's guidance for the first time.

Lights on. Float for the day from the safe in the kitchen. She counted the money quickly as she filled the register drawer. Start the computers. She checked the time. Half past eight—half an hour until opening.

Charlotte swept the polished floorboards, then vacuumed the large, dark red carpet in the centre of the shop that housed a reading island. At one end, two small sofas faced each other over a coffee table. Then, an eclectic mix of armchairs dotted the rest of the area, some with small tables at their side, others with reading lamps.

The bookshelves hugged the walls, and in a bright children's area, more chairs and tables but colourful and small for the little visitors. A box of picture books, well loved, was placed among them.

Charlotte collected a heavy-duty broom from the kitchen and unlocked the front door to sweep the pavement. When she caught her reflection in one of the windows, she paused.

Both hands on the broom, the woman smiling back at her was a surprise. Who smiles when they're sweeping? Dressed in a white blouse and dark blue pants, blonde hair neat behind a hairband, she'd have fitted in at an office except for the sensible black shoes. No heels when you're on your feet all day.

The outside of the bookshop was every bit as appealing as the inside. Windows on either side of the door each had four panes, separated by timber painted the same dark green as the rest of the façade. A curved canopy proclaimed *Kingfisher Falls Book Shop*.

"Are you open?"

A young woman with a pram had come along the pavement from behind her. With a smile, Charlotte went to the front door. "We are. Please, come on in."

By the time Rosie was expected in, Charlotte had served what felt like an endless procession of customers, gift wrapped five books, and introduced herself to several curious customers. During a brief lull, she latched the door open to let the cooler air from the earlier storm flow in.

"There you are, Mr Chen. Two beautiful gifts for your wife and daughter and all you need to do is add a card to each and put them under your tree."

Charlotte handed a gift bag to a middle-aged man in a suit.

"You've been most helpful. Tell Rosie she's done well."

"Tell her yourself." Rosie grinned from the doorway as she wheeled herself in. Grey-streaked brown hair pulled up in a messy bun, large glasses over sparkling eyes, Rosie's face might be lined, but its genuine warmth made it beautiful.

"Hello, Rosie. What time do you call this, young lady?" Mr Chen laughed.

"I call it about time. What would you like to share about Charlie?"

Charlotte shook her head and went to tidy the shelves as they chatted for a moment or two. In the past week, almost all the customers were delightful, a few curious about her appearance, and the odd one or two quite stand-offish. Not much different from her reception in River's End at the beginning of the year. Small towns.

Mr Chen left, and Rosie navigated her wheelchair to Charlotte's side. "Everything looks wonderful, Charlie. No issues opening?"

"Not a one. So busy though!"

"Close to a week before Christmas, darling. Before we get too busy, I'd love a hand refreshing the windows."

"I've never seen window displays as gorgeous as yours."

Both windows were used for showcasing new books, or a theme. Charlotte couldn't imagine making either of them better than they were right now, with their decorations and lights.

"Uh oh." Rosie glanced at the front door. "Looks like the ladies from the book club are heading in. Smile. No matter what, just smile!"

"They look harmless."

The slightly evil tone of Rosie's laugh sent a small shiver up Charlotte's spine. As Rosie wheeled toward the group, Charlotte pulled back her shoulders and smiled.

CHAPTER TWO

For the first time, Charlotte understood exactly how useful her doctorate in psychiatry was. The book club ladies were anything but harmless.

"I truly miss Braden." Marguerite Browne complained as she looked Charlotte up and down. "Such a sweet, polite young man."

I'll show you sweet. With a side dish of polite.

"He sounds like a nice person." Charlotte's smile didn't waver.

"What bookshops have you worked in before here? What qualifications do you hold?"

"Marguerite, don't worry about the new help, come and see the book I told you about." That was Mrs Octavia Morris, who Rosie had introduced as Octavia and was quickly corrected to Mrs Morris. Rosie simply nodded and smiled.

Only Glenys Lane showed any manners, but they'd already met when Charlotte visited with Trev. Mistaking Charlotte for Rosie's assistant, she'd purchased a stack of books on Charlotte's recommendation. Rosie had been amused, particularly as Glenys usually browsed in the bookshop then borrowed from the library.

The three women huddled around a new release in the reading area.

"Right, how are you at decorating Christmas trees?" Back at the counter, Rosie kept an eye on the ladies. "I want to replace the artificial tree in the window with a real one."

"As in, a cut tree?"

"Potted. That way we can plant it once Christmas is over."

"Oh, I love that idea! And to answer, I've never decorated one."

Rosie's eyes widened. "Never?"

"But, I'm a fast learner. If you don't mind me needing some direction."

"It will be my pleasure. Our tree will arrive soon, so would you remove the decorations from the one in the window? There's a box in the storeroom."

As Charlotte removed each decoration, she tried to memorise its place on the tree. The ornaments were beautiful, gold and red in two sizes. So simple but effective. The tree was empty by the time a small flatbed truck pulled up outside. In red letters across the side were the words 'Christmas Tree Farm' and a phone number.

"That's young Darcy getting out. His family started the farm more than fifty years ago and he took over a few months back."

Darcy was in his late twenties, thickset and smiling as he wandered in. Freckles covered his face beneath short red hair. "Morning, Rosie."

"Hello, Darcy. Darcy, this is Charlotte Dean, who has come to work with me. Charlie, please meet Darcy Forest."

They shook hands as Darcy grinned. "And it is fine to point out I own a tree farm with the surname of Forest. Everyone does."

"Didn't occur to me." Charlotte lied.

"Darcy, would you help Charlie remove the artificial tree from the window?"

"Sure. Actually, tell me where it goes, and I'll do it and set up the other one. Looks like you're needed." He nodded toward Marguerite, who had stood and was waving.

For an instant, Charlotte considered simply waving back. She hoped these so-called ladies treated Rosie with more respect than they were showing today. She hurried over.

"Mrs Browne, how may I help?"

Marguerite looked put out. "I'd expected Rosie to help us."

"She asked me to look after you."

Smile.

"But you probably don't know."

"Charlotte was most helpful when we first met." Glenys said. "She put me onto…" her voice lowered to a loud whisper, "Misti McCann's books. You know!"

The other two women reddened. Charlotte remembered suggesting a rather steamy mystery novel to Glenys and warning her to read the blurb first. From the look of things, she'd shared it around.

"Very well, what do you know about the author of this new release? We are considering this for our book of the month in January."

For a few minutes, Charlotte answered questions and made suggestions. Darcy emerged from the window with a large box, presumably holding the disassembled tree. Hiking it onto a shoulder, he headed for the storeroom. As he passed, his smile disappeared as he saw Octavia, who glared at him.

What's that about?

Charlotte excused herself as soon as she could and joined Rosie at the counter as Darcy returned. She watched closely and again, there was that glare, and pursed lips, from the woman. Rosie tapped her arm and shook her head slightly.

"Thanks, Darcy. Will your tree fit in the same spot?" Rosie wheeled around the counter. "We can make a bit more space."

"Nope, think that'll be perfect. Two secs and I'll have it in."

His smile was back as he went out to his truck.

"Charlie, give him a hand and I'll keep the book club ladies busy."

Darcy was in the truck, removing a pottery plate from a box. "Oh, I'm fine if you need to do stuff."

"Happy to help. Is this to go down first? Anything else under it?"

"It is a bit heavy, if you're sure? And I've already put a rubber mat down so this goes on top."

Plate on the rubber mat, Charlotte stepped back as Darcy carried a dark green pine tree in as though it weighed nothing. He placed it down with surprising gentleness, ensuring the pot didn't damage the plate. Then, he fanned the branches until it was full. "Being in the window, it'll need regular watering, but watch it doesn't overflow."

They left the window. The book club ladies were at the door, still chatting amongst themselves. Rosie was behind the counter and Darcy stopped for a moment. "Let me know after Christmas what day suits and I'll move it for you."

"Thank you, Darcy. It is a lovely tree." The corners of Rosie's mouth lifted.

"Shouldn't be using real trees, if you ask me. What about our environment?" Octavia had her hands on her hips, scowling at Darcy.

He slipped past the ladies and back to his truck without a word.

"For many years, my husband and I bought a potted pine, and every year it was donated after Christmas to where it was most needed. I'm doing this again because the farm needs our support, and it seems quite environmentally friendly. To me." Rose spoke with a calm tone, but her fingers tapped the sides of the wheelchair.

"But most of the trees from that...that place, are cut down, so you tell me how that is a good thing?" With that, Octavia flounced out, the others trailing behind.

Charlotte didn't know what to make of it all. River's End had its share of quirky people, but this little town might just outdo it for odd people with strange ideas.

CHAPTER THREE

I⟶T TOOK ALMOST THE WHOLE DAY FOR CHARLOTTE TO DECORATE the tree between customers, answering phone calls, and forcing Rosie to take a lunch break.

"But I always eat behind the counter."

Rosie's protest lasted for all of one minute, then she agreed it was a lovely day to sit in the park and enjoy her sandwiches. Watching Rosie wheel up the road warmed Charlotte's heart. This wonderful woman had worked hard her entire life and deserved a chance to enjoy the sun.

Once the tree was finished, Charlotte stepped outside to see it as part of the whole display. She gasped. The tree was gorgeous. Overflowing with the ornaments, and lit from around its trunk, she couldn't believe she'd never put a tree up for herself. And even though she could come and look at this one anytime she wanted, she filed away the thought of buying something a lot smaller from Darcy for upstairs.

Behind the tree was a wall running almost all the way behind the window. A picture of Santa with kangaroos instead of reindeer added an Australian touch. But in what she was beginning to recognise as true Rosie style, the flooring was covered in soft white fabric, and what looked like hundreds of crystal snowflakes hung at different heights from the ceiling. All in all, the window was a perfect mix of traditional and Aussie and it made Charlotte clap her hands.

Then, she quickly looked around to ensure nobody saw such an impulsive action. Impulsive and Charlotte Dean did not belong together. But the street was minding its own business, with pedestrians and cars.

Rosie joined Charlotte. She gazed at the tree, then up at Charlotte. "If this truly is the first tree you've decorated, then I've discovered a new talent. Well done, darling."

———

Although she'd told Rosie she was happy to close the store, Charlotte was secretly relieved to finish first. She'd not shopped at all since her first day here, only running out to buy the absolute basics and lots of takeaways, but now she wanted to fill the fridge and pantry.

Kingfisher Falls had two supermarkets. The closest one was also the largest, so after writing a shopping list, which was for everything except tea, coffee, and milk, Charlotte grabbed some reusable bags and walked up the road.

The pavement was still busy. People walked their dogs, or strolled hand in hand window shopping. Seeing several people outside the bookshop, looking in thrilled her. She pushed a trolley around, listening to the Christmas music as she put a lot less in than she expected. Too many years living from day to day. Halfway around, she stopped and told herself off.

This is your home now. And it is Christmas, so start acting like it.

She did a U-turn and started shopping in the fresh produce area. Lots of lovely vegetables, eggs, and crispy fresh bread. She wasn't a big meat eater, so chose some fish from the deli, along with a selection of cheese and ready-made salads.

Charlotte lingered over a display of Christmas cakes, shortbreads, and other goodies, then went looking for the more practical aisles with cleaning products and some extra plates and cups. She didn't need Christmas fare.

Walking home loaded up with her bags of shopping, Charlotte stopped at a few shop windows to check out their displays. The travel agency was impressive, turning the top deck of the cruise ship into an outdoor Christmas party. A ladies' boutique featured mannequins with Christmas attire around an artificial tree. But then she found one of Darcy's trees at a gift shop. Well, it looked like the one in the bookshop.

Earlier in the day, after the book club ladies had left, and Charlotte had finished the tree, she'd got coffee for Rosie and herself.

"You know I have no retail background, Rosie, so did I handle the ladies well enough? Or, how could I improve?"

Rosie shook her head. "They are the minority. All are a bit selfish and when they come in together, they make each other worse. You did great."

"I got the feeling Mrs Morris disliked Darcy. She was quite rude about his farm."

"There is a history. The Morris and Forest families were close, very close friends, until Octavia's husband…well, he took too much of a liking to the Mrs Forest of the time. Two divorces later, they moved away leaving both families shattered."

"Oh, how awful!"

"Well, you've met Octavia." Rosie smiled. "I've known her since high school. Divorce didn't make her that way, but she now has a grudge against the Christmas Tree farm."

Charlotte climbed the stairs to her apartment, mulling over the earlier conversation. Rosie had explained how Darcy came home from the city after his father passed away, bringing his own young family to a property allowed to deteriorate since the divorce.

She unlocked the door and carried everything inside. How sad that the poor decisions of one generation in a family were now impacting on the next. As she closed the door and locked it, Charlotte rested her forehead on the timber.

This isn't about you.

So why was her stomach tensed up? Time to stop worrying about the past. Being here was about making a new life. Not living with the sins of her parents.

———

In an attempt to lighten her mood, Charlotte played Christmas songs on her phone as she created a salad with a side of homemade chips. She made notes about which songs might be added to the bookshop's playlist.

The evening was warm, so Charlotte sat out on the large balcony to eat. Rosie had mentioned in passing that the apartment was built by the family who originally owned the building so they could run what was then a bakery and be close to work.

Imagine the smells wafting up.

Directly across the road, an alley ran between two old buildings to the next street. A car park was on a corner. For such a small population, the town sprawled with shops and cafes over four or five blocks. Further up was the small park where Rosie had lunch. Charlotte really needed to go for a long walk and get to know the town better.

What made the town special though were the decorations. Not only in the shops, but the streets. Streetlamps and trees were covered in fairy lights. At the far end of the main road was a roundabout and, in its centre, a tall Christmas tree. Artificial, but quite impressive with layers of purple and silver baubles the size of basketballs and a giant star on the top. At night, it was brightly lit.

Dinner finished, Charlotte washed up, yawning enough to decide an early night was in order. Perhaps a chapter or two of her book first. Or three.

CHAPTER FOUR

THIS TIME IT WASN'T A CLAP OF THUNDER ROUSING CHARLOTTE from sleep, but shattering glass. A lot of it. Not even bothering to find her errant slippers, she had the dressing gown around herself in seconds and was peering through the window. The sky was clear, and the main road was quiet. But she hadn't imagined the sound.

The silence was broken as tyres squealed and a motor revved. Charlotte sprinted to the balcony, wrinkling her nose at the stench of burnt rubber. Below, a car streaked past. A dark coloured ute, with of all things, a Christmas tree in the back, tinsel trailing behind. It turned the next corner with another screech and ornaments bounced down the road.

What on earth?

Charlotte stared back where it came from. Huge shards of glass covered the footpath and road outside the ladies' boutique.

There was no clanging alarm. Nobody else was around. And Charlotte didn't even know if Kingfisher Falls had a police station.

She threw on jeans, T-shirt and runners, grabbed her keys and phone, and tore down the stairs. At the bottom, she dialled police emergency, then headed for the boutique.

Emergency services answered and put her through to the police.

She answered their questions as she hurried there. They asked her to wait near the scene.

Sure, where else would I want to be in the middle of the night?

After hanging up, she checked the time. Three in the morning. Not promising for getting back to sleep.

She took a lot of photographs. Glass spread across every surface in the radius of the shop was from a full pane. There was glass inside as well, but she wasn't going to do more than zoom in with the phone camera. Charlotte searched on the internet for the shop but there was no website, after hours number, or even an email address to be found, only the landline. She dialled this in the hope it might be redirected at night, but after hearing it ring out in the shop gave up.

The minutes ticked past. Charlotte planted herself under a streetlamp a little further up the street. Running out here alone in a town she didn't know just after a break-in, was beginning to feel like a stupid decision. She could have called the police from the balcony. Instead, she was by herself with not another soul in sight.

The sound of a car approached. What if it was the thief coming back for a second go? Her heartbeat increased as the car came through the roundabout. But it was a police car, which pulled over on the opposite side of the road.

Charlotte shoved the phone into her pocket and began to cross.

The car door swung open. "Stay where you are!" A heavyset man in tracksuit pants and singlet hauled himself out, eyes on Charlotte.

Planning on shooting me if I don't?

Telling her sarcasm to stay quiet, she stopped as he strapped a police belt around his gut. If she was the perpetrator, she'd be long gone at this rate. He finally slammed the door and lumbered toward her.

"Is your accomplice inside?"

"My what?"

"Don't smart mouth me, missy. Who else did this with you?"

Charlotte rolled her eyes. "For goodness sake. I phoned you. The person who did this drove that way," she pointed. "in a dark coloured ute. With a Christmas tree on the back."

Up close, the man smelt of sweat and was in his fifties. Maybe older.

"Identify yourself." He barked.

"No. You show me identification. For all I know, you stole the police car."

Great. One minute in a new town and you'll be arrested.

She forced her voice to be calm. "I heard the glass break and phoned the police."

He looked her up and down. "I'm Senior Constable Sid Browne."

Browne? Surely not.

"Nice to meet you. I am Charlotte Dean."

"Did you say Christmas tree?" He crunched his way to the open window.

"There's ornaments all the way along the road."

Sid pulled a flashlight from the belt and stepped inside. "You sure nobody's in here?"

"Not at all. I've told you what I saw. I'm hardly going to interfere with a crime scene by stepping all over it."

"Crime scene." He laughed. "Everyone's an amateur sleuth."

"No, but I've been around crime scenes and there are protocols to follow."

"Like getting someone at this hour to clean this mess up." He came back outside, scrolled through his phone, and dialled a number.

He turned what Charlotte decided were beady eyes on her again. She stared back. His shoulders were hairy. Funny the things one notices.

"This is Senior Constable Sid Browne. Someone's broken into your shop, so I need you down here." He listened, looking bored. "Instead of having a meltdown, hurry up and bring a broom. It's a mess." He hung up.

Charlotte knew her eyes widened.

"What is it with you females? Hysterical over nothing."

"Right. I'll be going home now."

"I need your details. But I haven't got my notebook."

"Pity. Anyway, I work at the bookshop, so am easy to find."

Sid crossed his arms, his face even sourer. "So, you're the new girl. When's Rose leaving then?"

"You'd need to ask her. Goodnight." Charlotte walked away, not trusting herself to stay near the man for a second longer. She'd dealt with many police officers over the years through the course of her work, not only as an expert witness, but counselling people on both sides of the law. This was the first time she'd wanted to punch one.

And then there was Trev. The corners of her mouth involuntarily lifted. Rosie's son, and the sole police officer in River's End. And nothing like the one here.

Outside the bookshop, Charlotte stopped and glanced back. Sid still watched her.

Creepy, nasty man.

Perhaps she should stay to make sure he didn't bully the poor woman whose shop was violated. From the alley across the road, a sound, a crunch sounded. Charlotte pulled her keys out and climbed back up the stairs.

CHAPTER FIVE

"I HOPE YOU DON'T THINK THIS TOWN IS OVERRUN WITH MEAN people." Rosie handed books to Charlotte from the counter, where she was unpacking a delivery. "And most of the book club ladies are nice. I promise."

"Hm. Let's see." Arms filled, Charlotte tried and failed to count her fingers. "The meanies so far are Mrs Morris, Mrs Browne, and Mr Browne."

"Senior Constable Browne to you." Rosie grinned.

"Not in tracksuit pants and singlet. He's just good old Sid." She glanced around to make sure they were alone. "How does he have the job instead of someone like…"

"Trev?" The smile faded and Rosie busied herself. "He's been here a long time and finds a way to stay firmly entrenched."

"But we're not a country where local politics plays a role in choosing the police. Surely there's been enough complaints to have him removed?"

"Most of us just avoid him. Once you've put these on the shelves, please take some money from petty cash and run over to the cakeshop. I think a selection of pastries might cheer up poor Esther."

All morning, Rosie and Charlotte had taken turns checking

outside on the progress around the boutique. Much earlier, from the safety of the balcony, tea in hand, Charlotte had seen Esther and a short, balding man that Rosie later assured her was her husband, arrive. Esther had stood on the road, hands over her mouth until her husband wrapped his arms around her. At least she'd had another person there to keep Sid off her back.

As a glass company installed a new window, a car with a security logo had arrived. Once it left, Rosie said it was time to offer some sympathy and comfort.

"I'm okay to stay here if you'd like to go, Rosie."

"Actually, that would be good, if you're sure?"

Of course, the minute Rosie left, customers filled the shop. Charlotte darted between people with a word here, a book recommendation there, checking everyone was fine before starting over again. It was fun. Frantic but fun.

"Now, how may I assist?" Charlotte was aware of someone in the back of the shop but only reached them as they turned around. "Senior Constable Browne. And you are in the mystery and thrillers section!"

"I don't read."

"That's a shame. I have a new true crime book that is heavy on procedure—"

"I'm here to discuss the break in."

Charlotte glanced around the shop. They were alone. Even though Sid wore a police uniform now, Charlotte was uncomfortable. Something about the way he stared, the slight smirk, unnerved her.

"Happy to help, but if customers come in, I'll need to attend to them."

He pulled out a notebook, ran his thumb over a white-coated tongue, and flicked to a blank page. "I'll need your full name, address, date of birth, previous address—"

"No. I'm merely a person who heard a noise and then saw a car. I am not involved with the break in. My name is Charlotte Dean, and I live upstairs." She raised her chin, eyes steady.

"I think I'll decide what information I want, missy."

"I'm not going to argue with you, Senior Constable, so what questions do you have?"

Sid's beady eyes narrowed, and his face reddened from the neck up. He snapped his notebook shut. "Don't make an enemy of me."

"Hello, Sid." Rosie called from the doorway. "You look a bit hot and bothered."

He turned to go, then paused. "I'm going to find out what your story is. Missy." He sneered.

Charlotte kept her back straight until he was out of the shop, then she took a deep breath. She folded her arms, so Rosie wouldn't see her hands shake. "Well, he is a charmer."

———

A coffee and delicious pastry later, Charlotte had stopped fuming. Or at least, she'd relegated the powerful emotions to her 'later' mental file.

"Does he call every woman 'missy'?" she wiped her fingers on a napkin.

"No. But he generally finds something derogatory. We tend to ignore it, like you did. May I have that cupcake? I am ravenous!"

Charlotte pushed the box across. "Thanks for these. I'm sure Esther was touched with the box you got her."

"She's rattled, Charlie. And who can blame her? I can't recall crime like that...well, not for a long time. I wish Sid took it seriously."

"Yup. Not a question about the make or colour of the ute. Much more interested in my previous employment."

Rosie finished a mouthful, her expression annoyed. "None of his business. You're going to be a local, so he can take his questions and—"

"Rosie!" Charlotte giggled. "It's okay, I can handle him."

But could she? What if he did dig around in her past, particularly back to her life in Queensland? There were things she wasn't proud of, and whilst she'd never broken the law, some people believed she'd done something just as bad. Probably they were correct.

"Where's that smile? That doughnut won't eat itself."

With a fake sigh, Charlotte picked it up and looked at it from every angle. "Your son once asked me if I was a runner."

"Did he now?"

"I scoffed. Running requires a commitment to pain I just can't find. But..." she moved the doughnut close to her lips. "Many more of these and I'll have to take it up."

"He'll be thrilled. Give him yet another thing in common with you." Rosie laughed as Charlotte almost choked on her bite of yumminess. "Have another. I'll go and buy more."

———

She might have joked around at the time, but the memory of the whole conversation with Trev followed Charlotte around all afternoon. She remembered it so well.

It was the day before the wedding of her best friend, Christie. Charlotte was at the end of the jetty in River's End, a place most people seemed to gravitate to when they wanted to think. Or propose. Even break up.

She'd sat there for a while, reading, but also gazing at the ocean as the smell of sea air filled her senses. Trev was running on the beach. He'd gone up and down a couple of times before spotting her. Or at least, that's what she thought. They hadn't seen each other since getting back from visiting Rosie, and the series of problems he'd had to solve.

He'd stepped onto the jetty and stopped. Perhaps he didn't want to intrude.

"It's a public jetty." she called over her shoulder. A moment later, he was beside her. They did some small talk and she'd tried not to focus on his good physique.

Trev wriggled into a T-shirt and asked her if she was a runner.

"Not unless I have somewhere urgent to go to." She wanted him to believe that was the only time, but she did run sometimes. When things got too hard.

"You look like you do. Run." He said.

"Hot and sweaty? I'm teasing." She'd replied. "I have lucky genes. At least where body shape is concerned."

"What about the rest of your genes?" his question was innocent, banter, but it cut deep in a part of her she kept from herself, let alone anyone else. He hadn't noticed, but her fingers had gone straight to the elasticized bracelet she wore, worrying at it rather than say the wrong thing.

She'd changed the subject and things got awkward. They'd walked along the river that went through a rift in the cliffs. As they'd reached the road, Trev had found something to say. As if trying to put things right that really couldn't be.

"I spoke to Mum last night. She said to pass on her regards."

And that was when it hit her. What could be better than starting over because she wanted to, not because she was running away?

She'd asked about Rosie's bookshop being online. A thousand ideas flooded her mind to make it competitive in a market dominated by the big box stores. The more she talked about it, her enthusiasm rising, the more crestfallen Trev seemed.

"Are you okay?" she'd finally asked. "Does it make you sad talking about this?"

He'd encouraged her to follow her heart. It wasn't as though they were together, or even dating. But there was a certain something, a bond of sorts. And she missed him.

Whatever would he think about Sid?

CHAPTER SIX

THE FLOOD OF CUSTOMERS THROUGH THE BOOKSHOP SEEMED never ending. By the time Saturday closing came, Rosie looked as tired as Charlotte felt. Her feet ached, back hurt, and never in her life had she talked so much. Particularly not small talk.

"Enjoy tomorrow." Rosie went out through the back door, with Charlotte locking it behind them both. "Take the day to enjoy a rest."

"How far away do you live?" Charlotte walked around to the front of the store along a narrow driveway.

They stopped outside the bookshop.

"Only two blocks. I have a car but keep it for longer excursions. And shopping. Tomorrow I intend to start planning Christmas Day. You will come for dinner?"

A flutter of nerves played in Charlotte's stomach. "Oh, um, I hadn't given Christmas any thought."

Rosie smiled. "Exactly what I thought. Darling, you don't need to come along because I invite you. If you prefer a day to yourself, then take it. But I would love the company. I do enjoy Christmas, very much. You don't even have to let me know in advance, I'll text you my address and you can drop in anytime."

"Oh, thank you. I don't want to be a nuisance."

"As if you ever could be."

With a wave, Rosie turned the wheelchair and picked up speed. Charlotte's stomach settled, warmth replacing the flutters. She was unaccustomed to the kindness shown to her in the past year. Until River's End, she'd had colleagues and some close acquaintances, but never a real friend, the type who'd stand by you when you made big mistakes.

And have I made some of those.

Charlotte had no idea why she was worrying about the past when her present was so nice. She doubled back to the stairs and went to the apartment. After a long glass of water, she changed into shorts and T-shirt and runners. A walk around town was exactly what she needed.

Half the town had the same idea. As she wandered along the main street, Charlotte recognised a few people who'd been into the bookshop. Some said hello, others hurried past with bags of shopping. Kingfisher Falls was almost three times the size of River's End, but still very much a small town. She'd only explored the main street, so followed the footpath around the corner.

Even prettier than the main street, this was shorter but closed off both ends to create a plaza. Christmas lights were strung from one side to the other and changed from red to green to gold. A roving Santa rang a large bell, attracting adults and children alike. He carried a basket of red envelopes and let everyone help themselves.

Charlotte accepted one from him as he passed, thanking him. He ignored her, ho-ho-ho-ing as he walked away. Inside the envelope was a gift voucher to a department store. She recognised the address as being the next town. A large town closer to the city.

"Excuse me, Santa?" Charlotte ran after him.

He glanced up but kept walking, so she adjusted her pace to his.

"Hi Santa, or whoever is in there."

Santa stopped to ring his bell a few times and Charlotte waited until more of the envelopes were in the hands of locals. He stalked off again.

"I'm guessing you are employed by the department store to hand these out."

"So?"

"Bit unfair to the local traders here. Taking business away at the most important time of year."

"Take it up with management."

"Can you give me the name of someone?"

"Yeah. Rudolph. Care of North Pole. Now leave me alone."

Santa rang his bell in Charlotte's face.

She gave him her sweetest smile and wandered away. On Monday she'd talk to Rosie about this. It was a clever idea, one the town itself should be doing to support its own traders.

In the centre of the plaza was a fountain. Kids played in it, giggling and splashing water around. There were benches all around where parents sat. In the fountain, lights changed colour and reminded Charlotte of the much smaller one at Palmerston House, where she'd lived.

The end of the road turned into parklands. On either corner was a restaurant. One was Italian, with red and white tablecloths on its outside tables and the delicious smell of pizza making Charlotte's stomach growl. On the other side, and just as busy, an Indian restaurant added spicy fragrances to the air.

"Oh, yum." Charlotte murmured. She'd had every intention of cooking after doing so much shopping, but now, all she longed for was to sit outside and enjoy a meal made by someone else, and people watch. Italian or Indian?

———

Indian won. Charlotte scooped up the last of her korma with some naan bread. She sipped on a mango lassi, so cooling after the curry. By the time she'd finished, it was almost dark.

After paying and thanking her hosts, Charlotte went to the fountain. Not many people were around now, so she sat on one of the benches to watch the lights change beneath the bubbling water.

"May I join you?"

A petite, dark haired woman in her forties stood a few feet away, arms around herself. Charlotte was sure she knew who this was from seeing her at a distance.

"Of course, are you Esther?" Charlotte moved across to make room.

"Oh, yes, I am. And you are Rosie's new assistant." Esther perched on the edge of the seat.

"I'm Charlotte Dean. Or Charlie. I'm so terribly sorry about the break-in. Do you know what was stolen?"

"One Christmas tree and decorations. Nothing else."

"No money or clothes? My goodness, what a lot of effort for a tree."

"Replacing that window just took any profit I might have made this week. But that isn't why I stopped here. I wanted to thank you for trying to help. Going out at that hour to stand by the open shop..." Esther's voice faltered, and her eyes teared up.

"Anyone would do the same. I can't stand crime and you didn't deserve this." Charlotte went into Dr Dean mode. "This was done to you, and none of it is your fault. I think whoever did this will be caught and then—"

"No, they won't be." Despite interrupting, Esther's voice was quiet, her head down. "Sid didn't even take photos or fingerprints. He told us to clean up and he'd file a report. Nothing ever changes."

Charlotte opened her mouth and closed it. She'd pegged Sid as chauvinistic and lazy, but this went beyond a joke. She pulled her phone out. "I took photos. Can't help with fingerprints, and if nothing was found at the scene that might have broken the window then they brought it with them and took it again." She flicked through the gallery. "But you'll need these for the insurance claim at the least."

"I can't believe you did this. When we got there, we didn't even think about claims, just doing what Sid said. But without a witness, who'll believe us?"

"I didn't see what happened, but I'm happy to tell anyone what I saw afterwards. A dark ute with the tree in the open back flying past my place. They took the next right. And I heard the glass break. I've got time stamps on the photos. Where would you like me to send them?"

Esther swapped phone numbers and Charlotte sent the images to her.

"You said a dark ute? Do you know what make?"

"Cars aren't my thing. Sorry. Might know if I see it again. Does it sound familiar?"

With a shake of her head, Esther stood. "I couldn't say. Anyway, there's so many of them around here."

Can't say, or won't?

Charlotte got up. "Are you going back to the shop?"

"No. I'm waiting to meet Doug. My husband. He's a chef at Italia. Just saw you and had to say thanks. I'll run along now."

Something was very wrong in Kingfisher Falls. Charlotte didn't know what was going on, but there was more to this break in than a simple desire to take a Christmas tree.

CHAPTER SEVEN

CHARLOTTE WORK UP A LITTLE AFTER SEVEN THE NEXT MORNING, checking the clock twice. How pleasant to sleep in. No thunder, nor breaking glass. Before settling down, she'd checked all the doors were locked and turned off all the lights. Tiredness from too many nights of interrupted sleep kicked in the moment she climbed into bed.

After a shower, she took the time to cook breakfast and enjoy coffee on the balcony. The town was quiet and the sky blue, without much heat in the air. From here, the hills were a pretty backdrop to Kingfisher Falls, enticing her with the promise of winding roads and interesting places to discover. She'd collected a map of the area from downstairs, preferring to pore over a real one than cope with those on her phone.

Within a few kilometres radius there were three other towns. Hanging Rock was a little further away and she decided to leave that for another day. She'd always been intrigued by the story of the curious schoolgirls who disappeared there, not that it was a true story. Or was it?

She tossed sunscreen, phone, keys, wallet, and hat into a bag, then carefully backed her car from the garage at the back of the driveway and turned onto the street. She'd memorised the way to her first stop. Her fingers tapped the steering wheel in time to an upbeat song as she drove out of town, to an unexplored place.

The road climbed gradually until as Charlotte rounded a bend, the town was below her. How beautiful it was, with willows following a long creek on one side, and the town on the other. A moment later, the sign for the Christmas Tree farm sent her along a side road. What began as tarmac changed to gravel and she slowed to reduce dust and stones flying everywhere. The road narrowed and she was unsure whether to turn around or keep going.

But then a big, bright sign on one side declared she'd reached the Christmas Tree farm, and with a small sigh of relief, she followed the driveway. Pine trees of varying sizes were on either side as far as the eye could see, and their fresh smell replaced the dusty one from a moment before. She pulled to one side to let a car and trailer with a tree tied on it pass from the other direction.

The driveway opened into a huge carpark. There was an old, two storey house at the bottom and on the far side some sheds, where the main activity was going on. She parked and turned off the motor. The buzz of a chainsaw was somewhere nearby amongst the trees, reminding Charlotte that Octavia had accused Darcy of damaging the environment by cutting trees down.

Charlotte locked the car, then wandered across to the shed, stopping twice as cars with laden trailers passed her. One open-sided building had a sign at the front. *Sales.* Just behind that was an area with potted trees.

All were too large for her. There was plenty of room in her house for even the larger trees, but all she wanted was something small to go on the balcony. Right at the back, a smaller tree was on its side, and she righted it.

Its branches were sparse, and some had browned on the ends. Perhaps this was a reject. She poked the dried-out soil in the pot.

"Whatcha doing?"

Straightening up, she looked around. A boy of around seven or eight stood staring at her with his arms crossed. He wore oversized gumboots, shorts and a large, floppy hat, and a T-shirt proclaiming, 'Christmas Tree Farm Official Helper'.

"Hello. I'm Charlotte."

"That tree's kinda dead."

"I like it. And I think it just needs a bit of water and sunshine."

"You some kind of tree doctor?" he stepped a bit closer to peer at the pot. "I think it's dead."

"I might buy it anyway and take a chance on it." Charlotte bent to pick it up but the boy grabbed it first.

"I'll take it for you. Man's gotta earn a living." He wrapped both arms around the pot and raised it with a grunt. The tree wobbled around as he carried it through to the shed. A young woman, heavily pregnant, sat behind a long trestle table. On one end were a series of open boxes with ornaments for sale, and then rows of tinsel.

"Here we go." The boy placed the tree in front of the table and spoke to the woman. "Customer, Mrs Forest."

"Thanks, Lachie. But it really is fine to call me Mum."

Charlotte hid a smile at Lachie's serious response. "No can do, Mrs Forest."

"Okay, then. Oh, but that one looks almost dead. Let's find you something better." Mrs Forest began to push herself to her feet.

"I quite like it. I'm a bit of a fixer." Charlotte held out her hand. "I'm Charlotte."

"I'm Abbie. You're Rosie's new assistant."

Small towns.

"I am. And I really just want a little tree to put on the balcony, so this one is perfect."

Abbie settled again, frowning. "If you're sure. But I can't charge you for it."

"I'd feel better if you do, Abbie. You've put money into growing it. And I need ornaments. I've never had my own tree!"

Charlotte spent a few minutes selecting ornaments and tinsel. A few trees were sold as she browsed, mostly cut trees going straight onto trailers. Darcy waved as he helped lift and secure a tree. After Charlotte paid—which was much less than she thought she should pay—Lachie again hauled the tree into his arms and led the way to her car.

"I imagine Mum and Dad love having you help out." Charlotte opened the back door and helped Lachie set the pot on the floor. The tree came up to the roof.

"Mum can't...I mean, Mrs Forest can't lift much so I'm being Mr Forest's right hand man."

"Bet you'll get something extra nice from Santa."

Lachie gave her a stern look. "Santa is for little kids." But then he sighed and looked down, kicking at the gravel. "Dad says us being together as a family is all we need for Christmas."

Oh, sweetheart.

"Your dad is a wise man. Thanks for helping me, Lachie."

Without another word, Charlotte climbed into the car. Looking at the little boy walking back to the shed, she needed the time to blink away unwanted tears before she started the car.

———

Back on the gravel road, Charlotte hugged the side as more cars headed to the farm. Lachie had hit a nerve. Or two. The other day, Rosie mentioned the farm was struggling, so perhaps Darcy was preparing his son for a quiet Christmas.

Lots of kids have nothing for Christmas. Lots of families are apart at this time of year.

Charlotte eased the tight grip she had on the steering wheel. Her body was tense, but she couldn't pull over along here to stop and do some deep breathing.

A car loomed behind and it took a second for Charlotte to recognise it was a police car. And with its lights on. She crawled to a standstill on the very edge of the road and the police car parked right behind. One by one, Charlotte unclenched her fingers and by the time Sid lumbered to her door, she managed a questioning smile.

"You're driving too slowly for the conditions. Probably cause an accident. Been drinking?"

Not so much as hello.

"Not much of a drinker, Sid. Particularly not in the morning."

"Senior Constable Morris. We're not friends. Driver's licence." He held out his hand. More like a paw with hair over the knuckles.

Charlotte slid her licence from her wallet. "There you go, Senior Constable Morris."

He stomped off to his car and got in.

In the side mirror, Charlotte watched a dark car hurtle along the road, followed by a plume of dust. The driver was driving too fast and as his car passed Charlotte, stones flew into the air. One hit the windscreen with a thud. Dust covered Charlotte as she pushed the door wide open. The car was a ute, and it was impossible to see the number plates through the dust.

She coughed as she inspected a large chip in the middle of the windscreen. "Damnit."

"Watch how you speak to me, missy."

"I didn't know you were there. See this?"

"Probably gonna break the glass. I'd get that fixed." He smirked.

"Why don't you chase the idiot who just did this?"

Sid gazed down the road, where the ute was turning onto the main road. "Didn't see anyone. Sit back in your car. Gonna breathalyse you."

CHAPTER EIGHT

CHARLOTTE WAS TOO ANGRY TO CONTINUE HER TRIP AROUND THE region and headed home. Sid had kept her for almost half an hour, checking her car from top to bottom when the breathalyser refused to give him the reading he wanted. Then, he'd sat in his car with her driver's licence. Instead of marching up to him and demanding it back, she profiled him.

Definitely a bully, with a decent dose of narcissist. Probably insecure. Add the misogyny and superiority complex and he became a nightmare in this job. Out here, with few checks and balances, he'd run things his way.

When he'd eventually held out her licence, she'd been able to consider him with a little pity added to the mix. He needed help.

She parked in the garage, glaring at the chip in the windscreen. This was something she'd need to get fixed but at least she wouldn't need the car for a while. That ute though. What she'd seen beneath the dust was familiar. If it was the one from the other night, then she wanted to find it. Sid saying he'd seen nothing gave a whole new element to this.

Was he part of it? Or just knew the culprit and didn't want to do anything. Either way, he wasn't the person for the job.

And you are?

As she lugged the tree upstairs, she grinned at herself. *Charlotte Dean, Private Eye.* If the bookshop didn't work out, she could pursue the life of a private investigator. Smiling helped. Enjoying the small kick of serotonin, she grinned again.

At the top of the stairs was a small landing near the door. And a box took up much of the space. Taped on top was a handwritten note.

Was delivered to us by accident. Rosie told us where to find you.

Charlotte took the box inside first, then returned for the little tree.

The balcony was in full sun, with only one spot dappled by the shade of a neighbouring tree. Rather than shock the poor pine, she placed it where it had both sun and shade. It was so dried out that she poured two full jugs of water into the soil before it did more than run straight through the pot.

Back downstairs, she retrieved the ornaments and tinsel.

Sid Morris was still on her mind as she let herself back in the house. She flicked the kettle on, then lay on the floor and focussed on a spot on the ceiling as it boiled. Her heartrate came down, the anger drained away, and she regulated her breathing, flicking the bracelet to focus the emotions.

Need to meditate more often, Charlie.

The move to Kingfisher Falls, leaving behind the friends she loved in River's End, dealing with new challenges, all of this raised her anxiety. Which was perfectly normal. But it was time for some self-care.

She made her coffee strong and took it onto the balcony, which was quickly becoming her favourite place. From here she could sit unnoticed from the street yet watch the comings and goings of this small town. In the new year, she'd buy some new furniture for out here. Perhaps a little BBQ to cook with on warm nights. If only she could think of a way for Rosie to come upstairs, she'd have her over for dinner.

"You will come for dinner?" Rosie had asked that only yesterday. Christmas dinner wasn't something Charlotte had often experienced.

A couple of times she'd been invited to colleagues' homes, but it had been out of pity for her being alone. She was sure of that. She'd eaten and nodded and smiled, left a generic bottle of wine and flowers, then fled the minute she was able to. Somehow, the idea of sharing a table with Rosie wasn't as confronting. From the moment they'd met, Rosie and Charlotte clicked. Maybe she'd let Rosie know she'd be along, and even offer to come early and help.

———

Charlotte stared at the box. It stared back. At some point she'd need to open it, if only to discover the sender. There was nobody in her life who'd send a Christmas present. Nobody who'd know her address, that is.

Not Trev?

Surely, he knew better. Their relationship—if one could even call it that—was more a loose friendship. An occasional moment of laughter. Sometimes, a connection over a mystery. There she was again, back to being a detective.

Christie? Now, that made sense. Christie was the queen of mysteries *and* knew her address. But she was busy with opening her new beauty salon and being a newlywed. Of course, if Christie knew her address, so did most of River's End.

She found a knife and cut through the tape on the top. She wanted to know what was inside. Charlotte pushed the flaps aside and looked in.

At first, she didn't understand. There were books, and photo albums, and little trinket boxes, Christmas cards, and a whole lot of letters. And on the very top, in a plastic sleeve, an envelope. It was addressed to her.

Charlotte walked away. Went out on the balcony and played with the pine branches, whispering to them that they were wanted and needed to grow. She gazed down the road, not seeing a thing.

And then she returned to the box and slid the envelope out of the plastic sleeve.

Dear Dr Dean,

The board of Lakeview Care thought it was time to forward the remaining items Angelica kept from the house. With the deteriorating condition of your mother, we felt it prudent to send what is yours. She has held on to these as some kind of comfort but has not touched them in weeks. We believe it is safe to send them now.

Sincerely,
Maggie

Charlotte let the note escape her fingers and watched it fall to the ground. She walked to the kitchen. Then back to the balcony. And then, she collected a book from the pile on a coffee table and went to the bedroom.

CHAPTER NINE

THE ATTEMPT TO READ THE AFTERNOON AWAY FAILED MISERABLY. Too much was swirling around in Charlotte's mind, none of it welcome. After an hour of winding herself up even more, she decided she was hungry.

Creating a simple sandwich helped. The act of doing something productive let her brain clear some of the mixed-up thoughts and by the time she took it to the sofa, she was ready to work out what to do with the box.

Feet tucked under herself, Charlotte nibbled on lunch, eyes on the box as if expecting it to move on its own. Inside it were a whole lot of memories, and more than that, things she'd never had access to. The letters were from her mother, and to her mother. She'd seen them before but kept locked away in a box. And her mother didn't speak of them. Never had.

Half of her wanted to reseal it and send it back.

Coward.

She put the plate down, lunch only part eaten.

It wasn't cowardice to shy away from darkness if it scared you.

So, find a light.

Charlotte knew this was the right approach, but there wasn't any light she could shine on it. Not yet. The best thing was to put it out of sight until she'd found a metaphorical light. And she would. If anything, Charlotte was expert at clever ways to create shields. At least, she was for other people when she was practicing psychiatry.

This reminded her of something a wise woman told her. Back in River's End, she'd spent some time with Christie's great-aunt Martha, a woman who'd lost the love of her life and found him again. For many years, she'd lived on the other side of the world, with little knowledge of events in her hometown. The arrival of a box of her possessions, accidentally left behind, came as a shock and she'd hidden it in a broom closet for years. Eventually, she'd revisited the memories and found strength in the once-beloved items.

"Better to deal with a problem when it happens." Martha had told Charlotte over coffee. "Burying the past is the least effective way of finding happiness."

Martha's wisdom made sense. She'd find a way to take everything out of her box and inspect the past. Perhaps Martha would come and help her.

Charlotte folded the flaps down and carried the box into a spare bedroom. There, she left it on the bed and closed the door behind herself. Time to finish lunch.

———

"How pretty are you?" Charlotte stepped back from the tree with a smile. She'd been careful not to overload its sagging branches, but even with only a dozen baubles, the little pine brightened up the balcony. "I'm going to nurture you until you're strong enough to plant, then we'll find you somewhere special to grow into the tall, strong pine you are meant to be."

She leaned on the balcony railing, gazing up at the hills. Apart from some cleared land around houses, the hills were covered with all types of trees. Pines overlooked the sports fields, then deciduous trees such as claret and golden ashes. Autumn must be so pretty. Gum trees of different species. The beautiful golden wattles stood out against the green and grey of the other trees.

Movement down the road caught her attention as a car and trailer pulled up outside Esther's boutique. When Esther and Doug got out, Charlotte was relieved. Only them. And on the trailer was a pine tree, so they must have been up at the Christmas Tree farm. She watched for a few minutes as Doug untied the tree and then he and Esther carried it inside. How brave to continue and not allow the thief to frighten them.

And that's how it's done.

Shaking her head, she wandered into the kitchen for a glass of water. Hopefully there would be no more silliness in town. People had enough to do leading up to Christmas without worrying about break-ins or vandals.

This was Charlotte's first Christmas away from Queensland, at least since she was a small child. There were some vague, fleeting memories of a sparkling tree and a red ribboned present with her name on it, but little else. Her mother's progressive illness and refusal to treat it forced Charlotte to grow up too soon. Dad was long gone, and Mum had no interest in any kind of celebration. Besides, there was never any money so presents were restricted to those her school friends or kind neighbours gave her.

The pile of tinsel she'd bought glittered out on the table on the balcony. She'd not used it for the tree. But it would look great looping down from the windows. Charlotte grabbed some scissors, dug up some sticky tape, and scooped it up. This was her Christmas and she was going to enjoy every minute.

CHAPTER TEN

CHARLOTTE WENT TO BED HAPPY. THE LIVING ROOM WAS BRIGHT and cheerful with its tinsel, and she'd hung the remaining ornaments from the ceiling with string. It might not be much, but now she had a little touch of festive season in her heart. She read a new thriller for an hour, then slid under the sheets, knowing tomorrow was going to take every minute of concentration.

She woke at three minutes after midnight, her eyes flying open to see the time on the digital clock beside her bed. Why? It wasn't a bad dream, nor a storm, and she couldn't remember hearing breaking glass.

Go back to sleep.

She closed her eyes. From a distance came an odd sound. She'd heard something earlier exactly like it. A chainsaw. Eyes open again, she climbed out of bed and grabbed her dressing gown on the way to the balcony.

The sound stopped. There was no movement along the road. Esther's shop looked fine. The Christmas tree rustled behind her and she glanced at it. Just a breeze. If it was a bit windy, perhaps a tree had come down somewhere and it was being cut up to move.

The buzz began again. It came from near the roundabout and

Charlotte leaned as far over the railing as she dared. There was a lot of light there. But wasn't that normal for an intersection? And the tree in the centre had spotlights pointed on it from memory. The chainsaw stopped.

Laughter. Male laughter and raised voices. Charlotte's instincts went on high alert. She distinctly heard, "Pull, Darro." Darro?

And then a long, loud crack.

Charlotte sprinted to the bedroom. In less than a minute she was dressed and running down the stairs with her keys and phone. She sped along her side of the road, close to the shop fronts to avoid being seen. But she knew something bad had happened at the round-about. And she wasn't about to phone Sid.

She peered around the last shop on the corner. A ute and long trailer sat partway on the roundabout. Two young men dragged pieces of the giant Christmas tree onto it. Charlotte unlocked her phone and searched for the camera. Her hands shook and it took several tries to open it.

"Hurry up, Darro."

Whatever was going on, she needed to get evidence, so she snapped away as much as she could. The trailer had no plates and the men never turned her way, so she could only hope she'd got enough to identify them. The poor tree was in pieces, and one by one, the men threw them into the trailer. What wouldn't fit went into the back of the ute.

The same ute from the other night.

From behind her, Charlotte heard a car approach and flattened herself in the doorway of the shop. Ahead, the ute's engine roared and by the time the car passed her, the thieves were gone. All that remained were ornaments and a few broken branches.

This time, her phone call to the police was anonymous. Sure, they'd be able to find her if they wanted, but she had no intention of being Sid's prime suspect. Every instinct told Charlotte to get back to her house and mind her own business.

Like you're going to start doing that now.

She found a narrow gap between two shops and squeezed in. The roundabout was a mess with broken ornaments, discarded branches, and the ground dug up by the trailer and ute. This angle was better for photographs and Charlotte zoomed in to get more detail.

Sid arrived in the same singlet and pants from the other night. He parked where the ute was. So much for identifying the other vehicle from tyre tread. He kicked at a branch and squashed an intact ornament. Charlotte tried to switch to video mode and the phone dinged. She drew further into the gap as Sid spun around.

"Who's there? Show yourself."

Charlotte inched backwards, turning to her side to slide along the wall as footsteps approached. Cobwebs caught her hair and a squeal rose in her throat, but she forced it down for fear of discovery. Sid might shoot her if he found her. Who would ever look down this constricted space for a body?

"Is someone there?" A flashlight lit the entrance, then was directed toward Charlotte.

She kept moving until the gap suddenly opened to an alley and she threw herself around a corner. The light flashed where she'd just been, and Charlotte shoved her phone into a pocket and leaned against the brick wall drawing in short breaths. There was no way Sid would fit through the gap, but she needed to find a way out of wherever she was. He already thought she was guilty of something.

When there was no more light coming through the gap, she turned the flashlight on her phone on. The alley ran behind shops on one side and was wide enough for one car to drive along at a time. Cobblestones covered the ground and there were a few bins scattered ahead. Charlotte hurried in the direction of the bookshop. A few of the shops had back doors leading to the alley. The other side was fenced and from glimpses between palings, it looked like back yards of houses.

She neared the end of the row of shops. Ahead was the alley that opened opposite the bookshop. Phone in her pocket she crept along the wall to the corner. When she peered around, there was no sign of movement. The bookshop was in darkness, apart from the lights around the tree in the window.

Step by step, she tiptoed toward the street, stopping at every tiny sound. From here, the very top of her little Christmas tree was just in sight above the balcony. It needed a star.

Focus.

At the corner, Charlotte stared in the direction of the roundabout. Sid's car was still there. But where was he? He'd have to leave sooner or later, or at least call for assistance. A shadow passed in front of the bookshop. Sid was there. He'd been in the darkness until crossing in front of the tree. Now she knew where he was, Charlotte watched him until he'd walked all the way back to his car.

The minute he got into it, she sprinted over the road. In seconds she was around the back and flying up the stairs. Door locked behind her, Charlotte closed her eyes and exhaled. Too close. Far too close.

———

After showering to get cobwebs from her hair, and grime from her arms and legs, Charlotte was exhausted. She padded barefoot to the sliding glass door, towelling her hair dry. She'd left the door open, so began to pull it across.

She wrinkled her nose and stepped onto the balcony. Someone was smoking nearby.

The smell of smoke was strong. Charlotte stood at the edge of the balcony, scanning below. At the corner of the alley, Sid stared up at her, a cigarette between his fingers. When their eyes met, he sneered at Charlotte, then tossed the butt onto the ground and walked away.

CHAPTER ELEVEN

AGAINST ALL ODDS, CHARLOTTE FELL ASLEEP AS SOON AS SHE returned to bed and slept until dawn. She lay there for a while watching the sky go through all the hues of blue from dark to light, getting her mind ready for the day ahead. Open the shop after a quick check everything was perfect. Water the pine trees—hers as well as the one in the window. Sweep the pavement.

Oh, and pick up the cigarette butt in the alley. Charlotte couldn't stand the things being thrown on the ground where an unsuspecting animal might pick it up and become ill. Sid did it deliberately as soon as he knew she'd seen him. He was a dirty man on many levels. Butts, poor hygiene, and probably in his ethics.

Charlotte slipped out of bed and stretched, pushing the thought of the police officer away. Instead of lingering over coffee, Charlotte dressed and grabbed a shopping bag. She'd thought of a few things to add to her stash and wanted to have a look at the roundabout in daylight.

She went there first. No other shops were open yet, apart from the supermarket, but a couple of traders waved to her from behind their windows. It was nice to know her way around, and the doubts of her first week here were eroding. From the corner, Charlotte stared at the roundabout. Cars going through went particularly slowly as their drivers gaped at the empty space where the huge tree once stood. The mess was as she remembered.

Sid had done nothing. Nothing, other than act like a creepy-cop by standing opposite her residence. In between cars, Charlotte crossed onto the roundabout to look at the tyre tracks. Something made her take some more photos, quickly, so nobody saw what she did. Then, she crossed to the other corner and headed for the supermarket.

Charlotte found a Christmas star small enough for her tree, and a gingerbread house kit. The latter was a complete impulse buy and she grinned.

Much as she was enjoying the customers, Charlotte's stomach turned a bit when the book club ladies followed each other through the open front door.

Octavia looked her up and down and sniffed. Charlotte remembered Rosie's instructions to smile and kept smiling. If Octavia had an issue with her, then that was the other woman's problem.

Marguerite didn't even look Charlotte's way, but Glenys rushed over. "Did you see? Our beautiful Christmas tree is gone! Gone in the middle of the night!"

"I know."

"How do you know?" Octavia appeared from nowhere. "What do you know about it?"

Smile.

"I was at the supermarket earlier and saw the cars going so slowly around the roundabout. Quite shocking someone would do such a thing."

"Oh? I'd have thought you'd have heard something. Gone to check it out."

Was Sid sharing everything with his wife? "How may I help you ladies this morning?"

"We want to place an order." Glenys said. "We've decided to go with the book from the other day for our next meeting, so need a few copies."

"Of course. I'll get the orders book." Charlotte took off for the counter. The ladies were over in the thriller and mystery corner when she caught up with the open book. "How many copies shall I order?"

"We're talking! Kindly don't interrupt." Marguerite turned her back.

Charlotte considered dropping the book on Marguerite's foot but took it back to the counter. No smiling though. Rosie might be a saint, but Charlotte wasn't. She tapped on the computer to find the book to order. It had a longer than normal lead time due to the holidays and its popularity. That would make Marguerite even happier. Not.

She was right.

"Two weeks! We need those copies on the second of January. Not a day later."

Charlotte's fixed smile was back. "And if they happen to arrive in earlier, we'll let you know. Unfortunately, the wholesaler closes for a week at this time of year so all I can do is request these as urgent."

Octavia leaned over the counter. "I doubt that's all you can do. You're probably not even doing it right. How could you? You're not really qualified for this kind of work. Are you?"

"She most certainly is!" Rosie was just inside the door, her face furious. "Octavia, kindly let me pass."

Octavia's jaw dropped, and she stepped to one side. Rosie pushed herself around to Charlotte's side of the counter and put her hand on Charlotte's arm. "Let me say this once and then we'll move on. Charlotte is here because I want her to be here. She brings skills and a passion for books which has already made a positive impact to the bookshop. When I'm not here, Charlotte is in charge and I would take it as a personal favour for you all to respect that."

Warmth rose inside Charlotte. Nobody had ever stood up for her like that. Octavia's face reddened, Marguerite scowled, and Glenys nodded. Well, well, well.

Rosie removed her hand from Charlotte's arm and tapped the

keyboard. "Right, so the earliest you'll get these books is January seven. Perhaps next time you might need to plan ahead if there are any holidays. Wholesalers are entitled to a break the same as anyone."

She lifted her chin to stare at the three ladies. Charlotte stayed still and quiet. Rosie was a fireball in a controlled, polite way. One by one, the ladies looked away.

"Do you still wish for the order to be placed?" Rosie asked.

Octavia pulled her handbag closer to her body and huffed as she stalked out of the shop. Marguerite followed without a word or glance. But Glenys grinned at Rosie, then at Charlotte. "Please do order the books. We'll put our first meeting back a few days to accommodate the delivery. Thank you, Charlotte." Then she toddled after the others.

Charlotte sank onto a stool. "Oh, my goodness."

"That's all you have?" Rosie shook her head. "I am so annoyed with those women. Well, maybe not Glenys, but those other two!"

"What if they don't come back? I don't want you losing customers because of me."

Rosie turned a serious gaze on Charlotte. "Any customer who cannot behave in a civil manner can go. As much as I like trading, the customer is most certainly not always right!"

"Thank you."

"No. Thank you for keeping your cool and looking after my interests in the face of such rudeness. Really, I don't know where Octavia and Marguerite get their entitlement from. Ever since Marguerite married Sid, she's turned into a mean woman."

"I imagine marriage to Sid would do that. Coffee?"

Over steaming cups of coffee and a break between customers, Charlotte filled Rosie in on the events of the night. She left out a bit. No point worrying Rosie about Sid's odd behaviour, nor Charlotte deliberately hiding from him.

"So, two young men. One called Darro. A dark ute and a trailer. Surely Sid can find them based on that description?"

"I didn't exactly tell him. There's something else. He pulled me over yesterday near the Christmas Tree farm."

Rosie put down her cup and turned concerned eyes to Charlotte. "Why?"

"For existing. First, he wanted to breathalyse me and when there was no trace of alcohol, he inspected the car from top to bottom. Then he spent ages in his patrol car with my licence. And naturally there was nothing to find so he gave it back and let me leave. But in the interim, someone sped past and a stone chipped my windscreen. Do you know who might repair it?"

"Oh dear. I do. There's a nice mobile man so I'll find his number for you. Whether he is around or already having a holiday I don't know." Rosie searched on the computer. "Did you get a Christmas tree?"

"I did! It's a bit dried out and sad but I'm going to nurture it back to health."

"Was it busy up there?" Rosie wrote down a phone number and name on a notepad. "Here you go, give Ivan a call."

"Thanks. There were people coming and going the whole time I was there. I met Abbie and Lachie."

"How is Abbie? That baby is due next month."

"She's lovely and seemed well, not that we spoke for long. She knew all about me."

"Small towns."

"So I'm learning. Lachie is very cute. He calls his mother Mrs Forest and insisted on carrying the tree to the car. I got the feeling though that they don't have a lot. For Christmas."

"Darcy's father left him with a lot of debt, so I imagine money is tight. I do hope they have a good week. As bad as the Christmas tree thefts are, it might generate some income for them."

A family wandered in and Rosie greeted them. Charlotte folded the paper from the notepad. Esther and Doug had replaced their artificial tree with one of Darcy's. What would happen with the one from the roundabout?

CHAPTER TWELVE

SMALL TOWNS WERE GOOD FOR MORE THAN RUMOURS, GOSSIP, and knowing everyone. Charlotte's experiences in River's End was of a community that cared for its own, banding together in times of need.

Kingfisher Falls might be a bit different. Toward closing time, Sid strode in, along with two men Charlotte hadn't met. One was bald, sixties, sweating under a three-piece suit. The other also wore a suit, but no tie and the two top buttons undone. He was no older than thirty, with dark hair and shifty eyes.

"Gentlemen, how may we help?" Rosie stiffened the moment they arrived and stayed behind the counter instead of her usual cheery welcome from the customer side.

Sid stood back as the older man spoke after clearing his throat. "Ahem, good afternoon, Rosie. You'll be aware of the incident at the roundabout?"

"Yes, Terrance. Oh, Charlotte, this is Terrance Murdoch, one of the local council members, and Jonas Carmichael, another. Please meet Charlotte, my assistant."

They both nodded at her. Sid's eyes had not left her since he walked in. She gave him a bright smile.

Terrance continued. "Most of council are away on their annual holidays, so we've been left with the decision of purchasing a replacement tree. What would the town be without one?"

"Indeed."

"But council's budget is already spent, so we…well — "

"We need each trader to contribute to a new tree." Jonas took over. "We're trying to source one large enough and negotiate a low price, but everyone will receive a bill to pay this week. Council won't go ahead without every trader agreeing."

"I see." Rosie's hands were balled up. "Not all traders will be in a position to do so."

"Then they'll be responsible for the lack of a tree in our town." Jonas pursed his lips.

"Whoever stole the tree is responsible." Charlotte mentioned. "This is the second one."

"Actually, it is the third." Terrance nodded. "My neighbour came home from work last night to a broken back door and no tree."

"Was it artificial?"

Everyone looked at Charlotte.

"I'm curious why anyone wants to collect artificial Christmas trees."

There was a glint in Sid's eyes that turned Charlotte's stomach. What was he thinking?

Rosie crossed her arms. "Terrance, Jonas, this is grossly unfair. Council does nothing to attract buyers into the trading area. Now you expect us to foot the bill for something not of our making."

Terrance and Jonas exchanged a glance.

"Nobody wants to contribute, do they?" Rosie asked.

"A few have agreed." Terrance admitted. "Most say they can't afford it. Not sure what we can do, unless Darcy donates one."

"I think you'll get more local support, Terrance, if you ask him for the best price he can do, and then let us all know. And council has to offer some money as well to the pool. Nobody should be out of pocket at Christmas."

"Knew you'd take the side of those people, Rosie." Sid spoke up. "For all we know they are behind this."

Ah, that's what the look was about. You've twisted my words.

"Does Darcy have a dark ute?" Charlotte asked, staring directly at Sid.

"On about that again? How do we know you're not in with them?"

Charlotte couldn't help herself. She burst into laughter. Even Terrance smiled, but Sid glowered, and Jonas frowned. "Would you like to search the garage and my apartment upstairs? Happy to show you around. Where would I hide a giant tree, even in pieces?"

"How do you know it's in pieces, missy?" Sid pushed to the front, hands on the counter. "What did you see last night?"

"You are welcome to call me Charlotte, or Charlie. My name is not missy. Do you really want me to say what I saw last night?"

Go on, just goad me a bit more and I'll tell them you were watching me.

He pulled back. "We'll talk." Then he stalked out. Terrance and Jonas hurried after him, and Charlotte followed them, closing the door in their wake and locking it with a loud click.

"Charlie? What was that about?" Rosie wheeled over to her and took her hand. "You're trembling. Come and sit down."

"I'm angry. Sorry, he just really gets me riled up. He was watching the balcony from the alley. Made me feel creeped out, that's all."

Rosie released her hand, her mouth open.

"Rosie, I'm making things hard for you."

"My goodness, darling you are not! We should phone Trev."

"Trev? No! No, he'd drive up here and—"

"Exactly." Rosie sighed. "Alright. We're going to go back to my house and have a drink and we'll work out what to do next."

———

Rosie left first and Charlotte counted the money and closed the registers. She turned off all the lights before locking the money bag in the safe out the back. Still rattled, she double checked the front door was locked before doing the same with the back door on her way out.

She took a few minutes upstairs to freshen up. Rosie had texted her the details of where she lived, so Charlotte walked there. Past the roundabout—where several people had gathered—then on straight for two blocks before a right.

The street was narrow but pretty, with old deciduous trees forming an arch over the road. Rosie's house was the seventh on the left. It was white weatherboard with a colourful cottage style garden. A wide path took her to the front door, where a black and white cat sat in the late afternoon sun. A Christmas wreath was on the glass and timber door. She knocked.

"It's unlocked, Charlie. Come on in." Rosie called from inside.

As soon as she opened the door, the cat ran in, tail straight up. "Oh, um, a cat just came in with me." Charlotte closed the door, locking it behind herself. She followed the cat along a hallway with polished floorboards. Rooms were on either side. Dining room and bedrooms, all with their doors ajar. At the end of the hallway, a lovely living area opened up, with sliding doors to an outdoor area. The kitchen was to one side. The whole house was decorated, and a row of Christmas cards sat above a fireplace.

"This kitty cat is one of mine." Rosie was in the kitchen, the cat now on her lap. "Say hi to Mellow."

"Mellow?" Charlotte grinned and reached out a hand. The cat rubbed its face against it, purring. "Nice cat."

"Mellow and Mayhem. Siblings I saved from a fate we won't discuss. This one is a delight. Friendly, sweet, undemanding. Unlike her brother. Where are you, Mister Mayhem?"

With more a growl than meow, a second black and white cat appeared. He stalked into the kitchen and sat, staring at Charlotte with big golden eyes.

"I wouldn't offer your hand. Not if you value your fingers." Rosie carefully navigated around Mayhem, who merely watched her without bothering to move. "What would you like to drink?" She wheeled out of the kitchen and across to a small bar. "I have wine, most spirits, even some beer I always keep in case Trev visits unexpectedly."

"Anything. Whatever you are drinking is fine. How often does he do that?" she followed Rosie.

"Visit? Not nearly enough. Can't tell you how much I miss him."

A small pang of something resonated in Charlotte's chest. She missed him too. A little bit. "You won't move to River's End?"

"I love my life here. And one day maybe he'll get a posting closer again." Rosie held out a glass. "Gin and tonic, if that's okay. The gin is from Kangaroo Island in South Australia. My friend there sends me a case every so often."

Charlotte accepted the glass and followed Rosie, who placed her own drink on a side table and manoeuvred her wheelchair to one end of a sofa which had no arm rest. As Charlotte sat opposite, Rosie manipulated her body to slide from chair to sofa. She positioned her legs and picked up her drink with a smile.

"Now this feels better! Cheers, darling!"

"Cheers, Rosie."

Mellow jumped onto Charlotte's lap as she sipped. The cat purred, circled twice, then curled up, warm against Charlotte.

"Oh, she likes you! But if she's a nuisance—"

"She's a delight." Charlotte stroked the cat's glossy fur. "This is soothing."

"For you both. Now, I want to hear what really happened last night. All of it."

CHAPTER THIRTEEN

"He was waiting for me to see him. The way he looked at me turned my stomach." Charlotte had filled Rosie in on more of the details of the night, punctuated by sips of the rather nice gin and tonic.

"But he said nothing?"

"Nope."

Rosie shook her glass to release the last of the gin from the ice cubes and finished it. Mayhem leapt onto the far end of the sofa and meowed at her. "I fed you already. Stop complaining."

"Does Sid treat all newcomers like this?"

"I'm afraid it is more by association."

"I don't understand."

"There's what you might call bad blood between him and Trev. Not my place to discuss, but they've had words in the past and the fact you are here with me is enough to draw his attention. I am sorry."

"Don't be." Charlotte grinned. "I was profiling him yesterday. I came up with a long list of issues I could help with, not that I would. A person needs to want help first and I imagine he enjoys the little world he's created around himself."

"You've got that right! Would you make us another drink? I'm rather comfortable."

Charlotte carefully moved the now-sleeping Mellow onto the next chair and collected Rosie's glass. "You mentioned you knew Octavia at high school. What about the others?"

"Marguerite and Sid moved into Kingfisher Falls about fifteen years ago. She and Octavia hit it off immediately and when Glenys began the book club, they all became good friends. Glenys's lived here as long as I have."

After making the drinks, Charlotte handed Rosie hers. Mellow was back on her original chair and blinked up as if to say not to bother moving her again. "Fine, I want to sit on the other chair anyway."

"Cats have their own agendas. We simply do anything in our power to avoid upsetting their plans." Rosie was so solemn that Charlotte had to look twice to see the mirth in her eyes. They both laughed. There was a sense of happiness in this home. A contentment with life and enjoyment of her own company.

Charlotte gazed around the room. "This is such a pretty house, Rosie. And is that one of Darcy's trees?" In the corner near the sliding door was a dark green pine.

"Thank you. And it is one of his. My husband and I always took a tree each year and then planted it. There was a land care group who arranged places and the town area still enjoys the benefit our, and many other people's trees provide."

"It is a lovely thing to do. Once my tree is strong again, I'll find a home for it. Mind you, it looks better even after a few hours with plenty of water and a nice outlook."

"Yes, it's important trees have a nice view."

"I'm beginning to understand we have a similar sense of humour. Although I have quite a sarcastic streak I need to keep in check." Charlotte said.

"Feel free to be yourself around me. I do love my customers, for the most part, but there are days when being perpetually polite and accommodating is exhausting."

Charlotte reached across to the other chair to stroke Mellow. "Speaking of customers, have you ever had a wishing tree set up?"

Rosie leaned forward, interested. "Tell me more."

"Not that it needs to be a tree, but a place in the shop where customers might donate a book for someone less fortunate. They select a book, or one of our other gift ideas, and pay for it then we wrap it up and the customer writes a card."

"And we donate the gifts to those less fortunate?"

"Yes. The customer can either donate with their name or anonymously, and the card would include an indicator of the suitable age if for children, or genre if for adults." Charlotte smiled as Rosie clapped her hands.

"What a wonderful suggestion, darling! Do we have time to do it this year?"

"We'd need some signs, but I can make those tonight. And some little cards—"

"I have a stockpile of cards so that's an easy one. I wonder how we let people know?" Rosie sat back with a frown. "Too late for the newspaper."

"Will you let me set up a Facebook book for Kingfisher Falls Bookshop? I can manage it and get word out to locals. If you'll trust me."

"Everyone says I should be on Facebook but I'm not one for this whole social media thing. But wouldn't it take a lot of your time?" Rosie said.

"Not really. And once it's up and running, it will be perfect to put anything onto."

"Anything?"

Charlotte nodded. "Opening hours. Photographs of the shop. Images of different books. We can announce new releases and specials. Oh, and maybe have some author signings."

Rosie was suddenly very solemn and quiet. She held a hand toward Mayhem, who opened his eyes and ignored her. But Mellow hopped off her chair and climbed onto Rosie's lap as if she knew her owner was troubled. For a few minutes, Charlotte let Rosie think and finished her drink. Perhaps she'd overstepped her position.

Rosie wanted to retire, but even if Charlotte took over eventually, and it was too soon to know, she shouldn't be forcing her ideas onto the other woman, who'd successfully run the business for decades.

"Charlie?"

"Rosie, I'm sorry."

"Well, I don't know what for. I feel a little foolish for not exploring ways to expand our…"

"Reach? Grow the customer base?" Charlotte prompted.

"Yes. Our horizons, as it were. Please go ahead and do whatever you think will work but let me know how many hours you work outside your normal days so I can pay you."

Charlotte stood. "No extra payment required. That day I came here with Trev? I asked him if you had a Facebook page and rattled off a whole lot of ideas. So, I was invested then, and I am now. I think the free rent thing deserves a little repayment."

"Thank you. Are you leaving?"

"I'd like to get started on this and have a lovely salad to make at home, so yes. Please stay were you are though." Charlotte collected the glasses. "See you tomorrow."

———

Charlotte left after washing the glasses and saying goodbye to the cats, although Mayhem hissed at her. She stepped onto the street in near darkness. The air was warm with a touch of humidity. Hopefully not another storm. But there was a smell on the breeze and not a pleasant one. Cigarette smoke. Nobody was around when she looked up the street and down.

A few steps along, there was a lit butt on the pavement. Charlotte stepped on it to extinguish it and felt around in her handbag for a tissue. "Right in the middle of bushfire season!" she muttered, folding the butt into the tissue. She'd dispose of it once she found a bin somewhere. Holding it away from herself, she headed for the main road again. No point being upset about other people's carelessness. There was a lot to do this evening and, in a few minutes, she'd be home and able to write a list.

Almost at the corner, a prickle of alarm swept along Charlotte's spine. There were no odd sounds, no more bad smells, just a feeling from nowhere. She moved a bit faster and then at the corner, stopped and stared back down toward Rosie's house. It was quiet. No cars or people coming and going. Houses were mostly lit up with Christmas lights, adding to the festive feel of the town.

Charlotte decided she was over-tired from too many nights of disturbed sleep and dealing with a few less than pleasant locals. With a shake of her head, she hurried home.

CHAPTER FOURTEEN

LAPTOP OPEN ON THE KITCHEN COUNTER, CHARLOTTE PERCHED on a stool as she ate with one hand and set up the shop Facebook page with the other. Tomorrow she'd take photos in and outside the bookshop and upload those. For now, she did the basics and prepared what she could without images.

Next on her long list was to create signage for what she and Rosie had decided to call the 'giving box'. Rosie suggested covering a large cardboard box with Christmas paper and placing it near the counter, so Charlotte added this to her job to do, but this one for first thing in the morning.

After playing with fonts and images for a while, Charlotte was satisfied with the wording and appearance of the signs. They'd be printed in colour downstairs, then put around the shop and in the windows. Charlotte wrote herself a reminder to ask Rosie who would be best to speak to about the donations. Most likely a local church group or other care workers who'd know where a little extra would be appreciated.

Charlotte already planned to add a few books. Something told her the Forest family were putting their all into keeping the

Christmas Tree Farm afloat, so hopefully they wouldn't mind a couple of books heading their way for Lachie.

She got up to stretch and get some water. It reminded her to water the pine tree, so she filled a jug and went to check on it. This time it took less water to soak in properly, and Charlotte was certain the branches were a little more robust than this morning.

"You're going to be just fine."

She adjusted a bauble, then wandered to the railing.

A police car cruised past. Charlotte couldn't see the driver but was there anyone else but Sid in this town? It slowed to a crawl near Esther's shop, then parked a little further along, closer to the round-about. Keeping an eye on things? About time.

Before she could get riled up at Sid and his council friends, she went inside, locking the door behind herself as if to shut them out. If they couldn't—or wouldn't—do their work in finding the thief, then she wasn't about to do it for them.

Or was she? Charlotte came to a halt in the centre of the living room. Three thefts of artificial Christmas trees in three days. And the audacity of stealing the one belonging to the town. What was motivating the person, or people, behind it?

Charlotte returned the water jug to the kitchen and opened her emails. There was one person who loved a mystery even more than she did and was brilliant at solving them. Christie Ryan. She started an email.

Hey Christie,

I know you have your hands full but if you'd like a distraction, let me know and I'll fill you in on some odd happenings here in Kingfisher Falls. Someone is stealing Christmas trees, of all things! Artificial ones, or perhaps that is coincidence. And I've managed to put the local police offside by being my usual self.

As she typed, a new email arrived, and she stopped to read it. For a moment she simply looked at the sender. Maggie from Lakeview Care. Subject: Angelica Dean. What was wrong now?

She dropped her hands from the laptop, awash with a familiar coldness. As her own therapist, she recognised the response to seeing her mother's name. The coldness wouldn't go until she dealt with whatever this was.

Charlotte opened the email.

Dear Dr Dean,

I've left a message on your phone this evening but thought it best to follow up with an email. Your mother has recently begun asking to see you again. She's experienced a few episodes that lasted longer than in the past, requiring additional medication to manage her outbursts.

She reached for her phone. The battery was depleted, so she plugged it in and let it recharge. For a moment she stood at the sink filling a glass with water. It overflowed. Once she'd dried her hand, she forced herself back to the email.

Her illness is taking a toll on her. Some days she sleeps despite our best attempts to keep a normal routine, and then she wakens disoriented and the paranoid episodes begin.

Mrs Dean's deterioration since you last visited is dramatic. I would appreciate the opportunity to speak with you by phone to discuss several matters. Although I understand you are no longer in Queensland, please consider coming to see your mother while she still recognises you.

Charlotte closed the laptop with a click. Dementia on top of paranoid schizophrenia and other diseases was why Angelica was in residential care. A lifetime of refusing treatment drove everyone away. Every friend. Any family, including the man who'd bravely married a woman who turned on everyone, sooner or later.

Including me.

If she was treating a patient, Charlotte would know what to do. How to create a management plan and adjust medications and therapy to provide the most comfortable level of living possible.

60

But she's not a patient. Not my patient. Not now.

Charlotte was barely aware of grabbing her house keys and slipping her feet back into shoes. She was down the back steps in seconds and running. Running as fast as her legs would let her.

CHAPTER FIFTEEN

CHARLOTTE VEERED LEFT FROM THE BOOKSHOP, AWAY FROM THE shopping precinct and roundabout with its empty space where a pretty tree once stood.

Away from the broken glass in front of Esther's shop, the glass Sid saw not as a clue to catching the thief, but a nuisance needing cleaning up.

Away from the book club ladies who were not ladies but rude and conniving women with nothing better to do than question her right to be there.

And away from the apartment on the bookshop with its email from the place she'd sent her own mother to live.

Without slowing, she crossed streets for block after block until a narrow track took her away from the main road. In darkness she ran, not caring if low-lying branches of bushes stung her bare legs as she got too close to them, nor where she was going to end up. Her heart pounded in her ears until she knew she'd pass out if she didn't slow.

She staggered to a walk, then stopped, hands on her knees as she gasped in air. This was stupid. A stupid, primal response. Running away didn't outrun the demons.

Breathe.

Bit by bit, she slowed her racing pulse, sliding the bracelet round and around her wrist. She straightened and closed her eyes, reaching out with her senses to the peace around her.

One breath. Two.

She dug deep into her body with the calming mantra she'd perfected long ago.

One breath. Two. You have control.

Her fingers stretched out.

One breath. Good. Two. You are in control.

Her ears still rang. Except, it wasn't her ears, but a sound in the distance. Perhaps running water. A creek?

Eyes open again, Charlotte followed the sound, taking in her surrounds as she walked. The path beneath her feet might be narrow but was solid and smooth. On either side, trees and bush enclosed her. She glanced up and saw stars through a canopy of branches.

A small clearing appeared with a couple of timber benches and an information board. This was lit by a single solar light. It was a map of the area.

Kingfisher Falls Reserve.

Several trails forked out, one leading to the actual falls. "I didn't know there were real falls." She took a path that initially climbed, zigzagging around old tree stumps, and some ancient trees. Then there were steps leading down, with a sign warning they were steep. With only moonlight to guide her, Charlotte appreciated the rail on one side and was careful of her footing. Partway down was a sign to *Kingfisher Falls Lookout,* which now seemed a more sensible choice than going all the way down in the dark.

Charlotte gasped aloud as she stepped onto the lookout.

Around her, the trees gave way to a gully where a waterfall cascaded down sheer rocks to a pool below. Moonlight reflected in the pool. Charlotte sank to the ground, sliding her legs through the railing to dangle over the edge. Head on her arms on a rail, she soaked in the majesty of the falls.

———

As reluctant as Charlotte was to leave the lookout, the night air had cooled, and exhaustion racked her body. Her mind, though, was refreshed, and the anxiety and guilt were relegated back to their normally locked boxes in her brain.

There'd been no alternative to institutionalising her mother. Not after years trying to help her and failing every time. Charlotte had the skills to reduce the symptoms, but Angelica possessed neither the will nor interest to do what was needed. It was time to stop blaming herself for her mother's choices.

She wandered back along the path she'd earlier run along. On her next free day, she'd come here in daylight, bring a picnic and her phone to take photos. This might turn into her go-to place when the world got a bit too much. What a wonderful accidental find.

Ahead, the streetlights of the main road shone through the trees. Charlotte took a deep breath, almost ready to return to civilisation. The earlier panic was gone. Or at least at bay. Time to make a cup of tea and settle for the night. She smiled at the thought and turned right.

Straight into Sid Morris, who stood, feet planted apart, arms crossed.

Barely stopping before ploughing into him, Charlotte copied his stance, right down to the crossed arms. She didn't speak, merely looked at him with a raised eyebrow. Her heartrate was through the roof.

Not tonight.

"Explain your reason for lurking in the bushes."

"Seriously?"

"It's about time you took this seriously, missy. Since you arrived in town there's been trouble. And now I find you hanging around a reserve at almost midnight."

Was I there so long?

"I'm getting to know my new town. And I'm quite certain there was trouble happening before I moved here. Now, I'm going home." Charlotte went to step around Sid, but his arm shot out like a barrier and he leaned in toward her.

"You need to be careful." He hissed at her, his breath fowl.

"Don't think being with Rose will somehow protect you if you take a wrong step. Her and her son have no jurisdiction here and I'm the one who makes the rules."

It took all of Charlotte's self-control to prevent hysterical laughter exploding into his face. He really believed he was straight out of a western movie. Why bring Rosie and Trev into this? She sobered as she remembered she was out late at night on a deserted street with a man who hated her. One with a gun.

"I'm going to leave now." She used her best therapist voice. "There's no reason for you to suspect me of any wrongdoing. I'm just settling into a new job and not looking for any problems."

"Then stay off the streets at night. No more wandering around when you hear things."

"Great advice. Goodnight, Sid." Fingers metaphorically crossed, she waited and the moment his arm dropped, rushed past. Charlotte didn't look back or slow down until she reached the bookshop.

CHAPTER SIXTEEN

CHARLOTTE DID SOMETHING SHE HADN'T SINCE LEAVING Queensland months ago. She took a sleeping tablet. Since the events of the previous year, she always kept some.

Insomnia had taken over for a while during the worst of the board inquiry in Brisbane, and before she'd completely fallen apart, her doctor prescribed some. Two nights sleep and she'd been back in control and able to explain her decision about revealing confidential information.

Sid's threatening demeanour and apparent mission to catch her doing something wrong was the final straw on an already difficult evening.

She woke groggy and wanted to go back to sleep. But the tapping of rain on the window got her attention and with a moan, Charlotte slid her feet out. The sky was grey and the clouds heavy. Great when the weather matched the mood. Even a long shower followed by strong coffee barely made inroads on her disinterest in starting the day.

Second coffee in hand, she opened Facebook. Her cup stopped halfway to her mouth as she read the new bookshop page. More than fifty people had liked it. She had to double check. But yes, it was her page, for Rosie's shop. There were several reviews, all five star and suddenly, she was smiling. If a half-done page with next to no images got such an immediate response, what could they look forward to?

In minutes she was downstairs with all the lights on, taking photographs and uploading them to the page as she went, adding a description here, a sale price there. She searched a few local businesses, like Esther's shop and the Indian restaurant and liked their pages. Hopefully, word would get around as more people saw the new page.

After setting the store up for the day, she still had an hour before opening, so printed out the signs she'd made and placed them in high visibility areas. Now to find a big box. There was nothing she could use in the storeroom, so Charlotte headed for the garage. In the wall behind her car was a door to another room, but she didn't have a key. She found a wooden carton on a shelf. This would do for the moment.

Charlotte lined its inside with Christmas paper and mounted a sign on its side. She popped it onto a small table a few feet in from the door, where customers would see it as they entered. As a finishing touch she wound tinsel around the table. A few photos later, she'd announced the initiative on Facebook.

You should be proud of yourself.

She was. And a bounce in her steps replaced the dragging of her legs from earlier in the morning. This was better. A whole lot better.

———

"That is the third book in half an hour!" Rosie wheeled around the counter to deposit a gift-wrapped book into the wooden carton. "Customers are loving the idea!"

"It really is win-win." Charlotte was restocking shelves. "The customers feel good, the recipients will be delighted, and Kingfisher Falls Bookshop becomes a conduit. I loved your idea of putting five dollars from each donation sale into a cash fund as a little extra help. You are so generous."

"And you, my clever friend, are a genius. This concept is a

keeper, that's for sure. But this little carton won't cope if this continues."

Charlotte finished and joined Rosie. "No, it won't. Do you know if there is anything in the room behind the garage?"

"Oh. I'd forgotten about that. Maybe. My husband packed up what was left behind by the last owners. They left under rather... well, odd circumstances. They said to throw anything away, but Graeme couldn't bring himself to do so. He always hoped someone from the family would come back and collect everything."

"How long ago was this?"

"A long time. Way too long. Go take a peek and see if there's something we can use. I think the key is the little one on my keychain. After Christmas, we might get in there and see what's what."

The door creaked as Charlotte opened it. Just inside was a light switch and thankfully the light worked. She sniffed, then coughed at the musty, and rather dusty space. The room ran the length of the back of the garage and deep enough for shelving as well as a pile of boxes at the far end. The shelves were full. Suitcases, trunks, gardening tools, lamps, what looked like old cooking pots, and so many sealed boxes. Almost at the end was a large, rectangular cane chest. This might be perfect. There were clips on either end which undid with a bit of persuasion. Charlotte lifted the lid off, expecting it to be empty.

The sweet smell of roses and lavender wafted from red silk. Carefully, Charlotte moved it to one side. A teddy bear and bundle of baby clothes lay on top of a white dress. A wedding dress made of lace and silk, delicate and simply gorgeous.

"Oh, who left you behind?" Charlotte brushed her fingertips across the silk. She wasn't good with fashion, but this was perfect. And the baby clothes appeared to be handmade by someone who knew what they were doing. She adjusted the clothing and bear, covered them again with the red silk, and replaced the lid.

She stared at the chest. There was a sense of sadness here. Something lost. But she was being silly. Of course, it was lost. Surely nobody would abandon such things.

With a sigh, Charlotte moved to the pile of boxes and found one with only some old blankets inside. These she put on top of another box, then left, locking the door.

Outside, she shook the box upside-down. It was clean and solid, so she left it just inside the back door, out of what was now barely more a sprinkle than rain.

The shop was busy, so Charlotte tended to customers, gift wrapping presents, and adding to the giving box. Rosie was equally busy, and it was lunchtime before they had a chance to talk. Charlotte put the box on the counter and began covering it with Christmas paper before anyone else came in.

"Did you know the people who used to live upstairs? Oh, can you put your finger there?" Charlotte tore strips of sticky tape off a roll. "Thanks."

"Well, yes. But nobody really knew them, if you get my drift. You missed a bit."

"This was a bakery?"

"It was. A long time back though. This building must be eighty years old. The same family worked here for decades; it was generational. But Graeme and I moved into Kingfisher Falls thirty-five years ago. I was carrying Trev and we wanted a peaceful and safe place to raise a family. I used to come here weekly for a long time, but they were not part of the community type of people. Not the young generation."

"Is this okay?" Charlotte stood back from the box. The paper was festive with red bows and trees all over it. "Hope nobody thinks it is a Christmas tree and steals it."

"Funny. And it is lovely, so let's put it on the floor in place of on the table."

Charlotte shuffled things around and tossed packing paper from the book deliveries into the bottom and then a layer of tissue paper. "That's better, raises the books up a bit."

Rosie tapped the side of her chair as she thought. "There are a few people around who knew that family better than I did. Are you thinking of tracking them down to see if they want the contents of the cane box?"

"It must mean something. The dress is gorgeous, and the baby clothes and teddy were perfect. The kind of thing you'd pass down to your children, not leave behind. Did they go in a hurry?"

"Such a long time ago, darling. I seem to think they did. This place was for sale for a long time as a bakery. About a year. So, when Graeme and I finally got the courage to follow our passion and try our hand at small business, they were desperate to sell. I did none of the negotiations so there's a lot I don't know. I'm sorry."

"Don't be. I'm curious, that's all."

"I'm beginning to think you are more than a bit of a sleuth. Trev told me you like mysteries."

"Did he now?" Charlotte kept a straight face but inside, a little flutter played in her stomach. "I'm sure I have no idea why he'd think so."

"Speaking of Trev," Rosie said. "I might call him tonight to catch up. Anything you'd like me to pass on?"

Only that he shouldn't let you believe anything ever went on between us.

"Yes. My thanks for introducing me to you. Kind of like it here."

Rosie reddened, her lips flickering up at the corners. She looked out at the street and her expression changed to serious. "You may change your mind. Here comes Glenys. But at least she's alone today."

70

CHAPTER SEVENTEEN

THE STREAM OF CUSTOMERS CONTINUED ALL DAY, TO THE POINT where Rosie and Charlotte ate lunch in shifts behind the counter. One after another, people commented on seeing the Facebook page, until Rosie insisted Charlotte show her. She brought it up on the computer and left Rosie to look as Charlotte helped a small group of teens.

"Such a thoughtful gift." Charlotte gave them change after wrapping a book. "Your grandfather will love reliving those cricketing days. How wonderful he played for the state, you must be proud!"

She waved as they left then turned to Rosie, who was unusually quiet. The older woman discreetly pulled a tissue from the box on the counter and blew her nose. Charlotte watched her. Were those tears on her cheeks?

"Rosie?"

"Well, I don't believe I've ever seen my shop in this light before." She pointed at the screen, to a panorama of the store from just inside the front door.

"You don't like it?" Charlotte was afraid to ask. Had she overstepped?

But Rosie reached for her hand and squeezed it, still staring at the screen. "I love it. This will change things. Christmas is always busy, and January because the children need their schoolbooks not to mention the long holiday, so parents buy more to occupy their families. February is always quiet and last year the sales slowed so much across winter."

"I think we can change it."

At last Rosie looked up. Those *were* tears and Charlotte's own eyes got prickly and she blinked a few times.

"Charlotte, if anyone can change things it will be you. When Trev came to visit and you went off and sold Glenys those books, I had a feeling."

Before they both turned into puddles on the floor, Charlotte needed to find some balance. "Yep, Glenys will do that. And if you really want feelings, Octavia and Marguerite bring their own special brand."

"I know what you're doing." Rosie reached for her bottle of water. "I'll stop being all mushy now. What do you make of Glenys's visit?"

Relieved, Charlotte went back to tidying shelves, talking over her shoulder. "She likes to gossip?"

Rosie chortled. "Apart from that. Because she's always been a chatterbox, but never been nasty, and I thought her comments today were bordering on insulting about the Forest family."

Charlotte stopped what she was doing and wandered back to Rosie. "Obviously I know almost nothing about them, or her, or this town yet, but anytime a patient would tell me someone had brought it on themselves, I knew there was fear behind it."

"Interesting. So, Glenys starting off by wishing that the Christmas Tree Farm was in better state, and then that she was sad for little Lachie having to work at such a young age—"

"Having to! Ha, he's building an empire."

"He's a smart little boy. But what started off sounding like she cared changed when she said it really was their own fault. Did you notice her tone of voice even sounded nasty?"

"Or triumphant. Almost as though their misery takes away her fear. But what could she be afraid of from them?" Charlotte pondered. "You mentioned a bad history between the Forest and Morris families but how does Glenys fit into it?"

"They've been neighbours for a while. Glenys and her poor husband—God rest his poor soul—moved in up the road from the farm a few years back. But both properties are large, so they'd not even see each other under normal circumstances. I couldn't imagine what would make her like this."

Charlotte returned to the shelves, mentally adding Glenys to her list of Christmas tree thief suspects. Except her name wasn't Darro and she wasn't male.

———

Just on closing time, the blare of sirens filled the shop. Rosie and Charlotte hurried to the window as Sid's patrol car hurtled past, lights flashing, in the direction of the reserve.

"That can't be good." Rosie said. "I hope nobody fell down the steps to the falls again."

"Again?"

"There's been a few instances where people slipped and fell. The path is fine, but those steps haven't been maintained in years. I can never go further than the lookout because the ramp that runs alongside the steps has deteriorated so badly."

"Do you go to the lookout often?"

"A few times a year. It is such a restful spot. You should go there. It is nice in the early evening when all the birds are out and sometimes, if you are very lucky, a Kingfisher appears."

"A real one?"

Rosie smiled. "Yes. A real Azure Kingfisher, also known as *Alcedo azurea*. They're endangered in the region, even here in the town named after the species."

"Well, I shall have to spend some more time visiting the falls and watching quietly."

"More time?"

"I haven't been all the way down." Her stomach tensed.

Stop giving things away.

"Well, you should. Take a camera and a blanket to sit on."

"Sounds good." Charlotte busied herself in the window, replenishing some books they'd sold out of before the latest delivery had arrived. The friendliness and genuine warmth that was Rosie made her do and say things she didn't plan on. Too much sharing was the best way to damage a relationship.

"Oh! Do you hear that, Charlie? Sounds like a car chase." Rosie left the window to push herself outside and Charlotte sprinted after her.

"Rosie! Stay back from the kerb!" The roar of a car engine grew louder, and gears crashed. A siren was behind it. Charlotte stepped between Rosie and the road. "Seriously, what if it crashes!"

With a quick manoeuvre, Rosie backed into the doorway and Charlotte joined her, just as a dark blue ute careened around the closest corner, almost hitting another car as it skidded onto the main road. It righted itself and tore past.

Charlotte tried to see the driver but could only glimpse a male wearing a peaked cap. The tint was so dark it was impossible to identify anyone inside. Bouncing around the tray was a Christmas tree.

The police car was next, taking the corner only slightly less dangerously and pursuing the ute. Sid had a cigarette hanging from his lips.

Rosie and Charlotte raced to the kerb to peer down the street. Pedestrians stopped, and other shopkeepers ran out.

The ute barrelled through the roundabout, wheels up on the inside kerb and dirt spraying everywhere. Sid screeched to a stop as a car came through and shook his fist at the driver. By the time he got going again, the ute was out of sight, at least from the bookshop.

"My, oh my!" Rosie's hands waved around. "In our little town! Someone could have been killed with those two driving like maniacs!"

Charlotte had no words. Something didn't add up and she couldn't pinpoint it yet. There'd been no plates on the ute, and she'd had time to look, it was the same vehicle she'd seen twice before. No, three times before. It looked exactly like the one that chipped her windscreen.

Sid had said he didn't see anything, despite the new chip in the glass and the cloud of dust settling on them from the speed of the ute only seconds earlier.

"Rosie, did the ute look familiar?"

"I'm too mad to think about it!" Rosie wheeled back inside with short, jerky movements of the chair.

Charlotte wanted to reach out and help but didn't know how to without offending the very capable woman in it. She trailed behind and went straight to the kitchen. "I'm getting us some water." she called over her shoulder.

She filled two glasses with ice from the freezer and then water and added a slice of lemon in each. When she carried them out, Rosie was on the phone.

"Nobody should be racing along the streets of a shopping precinct, officer, not even in the pursuit of a murderer! And for all we know, this was simply chasing someone who'd stolen a Christmas tree." She listened, her face red. "Yes, you heard me correctly. Some person has stolen a number of Christmas trees from Kingfisher Falls over the past few days and it would appear our designated police officer requires assistance."

After setting Rosie's glass down near her, Charlotte perched on the edge of the counter. She'd never seen Rosie upset this way.

"You may laugh but had one of those vehicles hit a person you'd be investigating a different crime. Exactly. Very well, I shall. And thank you." Rosie hung up with more force than was required. "She laughed at me."

"Is she local? I got the impression Sid ran things here on his own."

"He does. This was a complaint line and I probably should have let it go."

"No. You were right. I'm pretty sure there are guidelines about pursuits in built-up areas, so Sid was in the wrong."

Rosie picked up her glass with both hands and sipped.

"You're shaking." Charlotte pulled up her stool and lowered it, so she was on eye level with Rosie. "That was pretty scary seeing the cars at that speed."

"You were right about me not being out there. I couldn't have moved fast enough if one had…" Rosie gulped.

Charlotte took the glass and put it down, then wrapped Rosie's hands in hers. "Nobody could. You are right to be angry about the risk Sid took in chasing the ute, but its normal to fear what might have happened."

Rosie licked her lips, then bit the bottom one.

"My heartrate went through the roof as well." Charlotte offered.

With a sigh, Rosie retrieved her hands. "I wish I had use of my legs again. That's all. I'm just feeling sorry for myself."

"Well, hopefully Sid will be questioned about his poor driving and he'll be the one feeling sorry!"

CHAPTER EIGHTEEN

Charlotte updated the Facebook page over a delicious dinner of pan-fried fish and salad. The page followers had doubled, and many people were commenting favourably about the giving box. After adding new photographs and reminding people how close it was to Christmas, Charlotte closed the laptop. She wasn't risking a repeat of last night with unwanted emails.

There was a tap on her door, and she froze halfway between the balcony and kitchen. Who on earth would come visiting? Before she could even call out, a folded piece of paper slid under the door. By the time she opened the door, the person was gone.

The paper was a flyer.

Who is stealing our Christmas Trees?
Meeting at 8pm tonight at the fountain.
The community wants answers.

There was nothing else.

It was almost eight now, but should she go? Her phone buzzed a message.

If you didn't get the note going around, there's a meeting soon near the fountain. On my way there. Rosie.

Charlotte collected her house keys and ran down the stairs. It was understandable the townsfolk would be anxious about the recent break-ins, particularly following the car chase today. Had Sid even caught the driver?

A group of thirty or so people had gathered near the fountain. Rosie was at one side where she had a clear view of two people who had dropped a couple of crates on the ground.

"Has it started?" Charlotte squatted beside her. "Who are they?"

"Not yet. The man with the grey beard is Kevin Murdoch. His brother is Terrance who you met yesterday."

"The councillor?"

"He's also rumoured to be Octavia's latest man friend."

This should be good.

"The woman is Veronica somebody or other. I forget. She owns the little garden centre just out of town."

"I haven't seen it." Charlotte said.

"Used to be owned by the nicest family but they moved on and she took over. She's never been there when I've visited though."

Kevin stepped onto a crate and clapped his hands. "Right. Let's get started." He waited until all eyes were on him. Unlike his brother, Kevin had some hair remaining which was styled in an unfortunate comb-over. Charlotte struggled not to focus on it, rather than his face.

"You may be aware of a recent crime spree in our town of King-fisher Falls," his voice boomed across the plaza. "No less than five Christmas trees have been stolen to date, including the beautiful one purchased by council at great expense, and erected on the round-about. Three homes and Esther's dress shop sustained damage during the robberies."

A few people whispered and from the sidelines, Veronica loudly shushed them.

"Today, our ever-vigilant police office, Senior Constable Sid Morris, almost caught the alleged perpetrator of these crimes."

Charlotte rolled her eyes.

Ever vigilant at hassling me.

"He was an idiot driving at that speed through town!" a woman called from the opposite side. A murmur of agreement rustled through the crowd, which was growing by the minute.

"As I said, Sid almost apprehended the criminal but lost him somewhere on the road to the Christmas Tree farm." Kevin said.

"Then it must be true!" A male voice from the back. Charlotte couldn't see from her position, so stood. It was Jonas, the other councillor.

"I've spoken to everyone who's had a tree stolen and guess what? Each of them replaced or plans to replace it with a tree from the Forests."

Kevin beckoned for Jonas to come forward and people parted to let him. He joined Kevin on a crate.

"Don't you all think it a bit suspicious that one business is profiting from all this misery?" Jonas asked. "At this time of year nobody has time to run into the next town to buy another tree, even if any decent ones are left. So, who are they going to turn to?"

"Oh, for goodness sake." Rosie's voice was calm and clear, and heads turned in her direction. "Has this meeting been called to blame one family for being in the right business at this time of year? Do you blame alarm companies as well when there's a break in?"

Veronica, who'd been staring at Rosie, stepped forward. "It makes sense. The Christmas tree from the roundabout simply cannot be replaced on short notice, except by Darcy Forest."

"Where is he anyway? Shouldn't he be here to stand up for himself?" another voice from somewhere in the crowd. People muttered amongst themselves. Kevin and Jonas exchanged a nod.

This was getting out of hand. Was Rosie the only voice of reason? Esther and Doug—wearing chef's whites—stepped through the crowd to the front. Doug spoke quietly to Jonas, who moved off his crate.

Doug took his place. "Look, I'm meant to be making you lot delicious pizzas and pastas, not running out here to talk some sense." He paused as a couple of people laughed. "But when our shop window was smashed the other night, we struggled to come up with enough money to replace the tree. And you've got to have one, particularly in a shop."

"So why not just get another artificial one?" Kevin asked. "Replace what you had?"

"Actually, we planned to. We'd got the last one from Veronica."

The crowd looked at her and she nodded. "I put them in when I saw how busy people were. Better to buy local, I say."

"And we would have, but your prices had gone up. Like, a lot up. Darcy's are much cheaper, and we got a potted one to plant afterwards. Keep the tradition going, eh, Rosie?" Doug winked at Rosie and she smiled.

"Well, I am quite offended you'd say such a thing!" Veronica was bright red. "I'm only a single mother who needs to provide for my children alone and pay my staff. There are overheads you know."

"Nah, don't be offended." Doug patted her shoulder as he stepped off the crate. "Everyone's trying to make a living. But we just couldn't justify paying double Darcy's price. Sorry. But he isn't guilty of anything."

Veronica stomped off around the other side of the fountain. Charlotte waited for someone to follow her, or call her back, but everyone was watching Jonas who'd returned to the crate.

"So, Doug has declared the Forests aren't behind the thefts. If I didn't appreciate his cooking so much, I'd have to ask him how he knows." Jonas waited for laughter, but none came. The crowd began to thin. "If anyone knows anything, or has any theories, speak with Sid. You can do so anonymously."

"Until he tracks you down." Rosie spoke under her breath.

"Rosie?"

"Nothing. I might go." She spun the wheelchair around and with Charlotte at her side, headed toward the bookshop. Jonas' voice followed them until they reached the road.

Charlotte gazed back. Only a handful of people remained. Kevin, Jonas and Veronica were in a huddle. "Shall I get some pitchforks?"

"I think it's all bluff, Charlie. Those two men like the sound of their own voices but it is unprofessional for a councillor to speak out against rate-paying residents and business owners. Thank goodness for Doug."

"Did you know Veronica sells trees?"

"Can't say I did. Really have only spoken to her once or twice."

"Do you mind if I walk with you for a bit? Need to work off my dinner."

"Can you keep up?" Rosie grinned and took off at speed.

"Hey! You got a head start!"

CHAPTER NINETEEN

O N THE WAY TO HER STREET, R OSIE FILLED C HARLOTTE IN ON THE structure of local council. Although most people, and even some maps, included Kingfisher Falls in the Macedon Ranges, it was its own tiny shire, bordered by Macedon Ranges shire on two sides. Its council resisted regular attempts to change its status, but Rosie believed it was inevitable.

"With the current lot of councillors, the mayor, and Sid, what hope is there of staying autonomous?" Rosie pulled up at the corner. "And now they want to chase the Forests out, I can't see anything but mayhem and sadness ahead."

"Mayhem and Mellow. That's who you should worry about, not the silly antics of grown adults who should know better. Rosie, I've seen people like this before and as you say, there's a lot of bluff. Shall I walk to the house with you?"

Rosie laughed, finally releasing some of the negative energy the evening produced in them both. "Do you know how long I've done this for, young lady? Back and forth, no matter what the season or the weather. Although if its wet or snowing I do take the car."

"Snowing?"

"At least once a winter, sometimes more. Now, off with you unless you need me to hold your hand."

With a wave, Rosie wheeled off along the footpath. Charlotte backed against a tree, out of sight, just to be sure Rosie was safely home before leaving. As much as she might encourage Rosie to not worry, Charlotte was. This town was a hotbed of corruption. Tonight alone, she'd observed more than one attempt to direct attention away from the people responsible for law and order and keeping the community both informed and feeling safe.

She saw Rosie turn into her driveway. Back on the main road, she noticed many of the houses had their curtains drawn shut. Last night, she'd seen into brightly decorated lounge rooms as she'd passed. How sad. The crime was taking its toll.

Was this some attempt to disrupt the town or were the Forest family being set up. And if so, why?

Glenys lived next door to them. But she was hardly hooning around in a ute. Charlotte needed to ask Rosie if Glenys had any sons or other young male relatives or friends. A 'Darro', for example.

The roundabout was ahead, and several cars were parked around its perimeter. Charlotte slowed, taking a wide berth but interested in what was going on. Darcy stood in the middle with a tape measure. To one side was Terrance, with Jonas behind him, on the phone and waving an arm about.

Sid was on a corner, arms crossed and legs apart, glaring at the roundabout. Charlotte found a dark spot between shops and waited. She was making a habit of skulking around in dark places. Possibly not the best thing to do when the town police officer was looking for any opportunity to make her life difficult.

Darcy finished measuring and waited as Jonas completed his phone call, making some notes on a pad. Did he know some of the townsfolk, including the man near him, thought he and his lovely family responsible for the tree thefts? If he did, how could he be so calm? Charlotte was angry on his behalf.

Off the phone, Jonas listened to whatever Darcy said. He shook his head. Now Terrance joined in, a bit more subtle with his response but still not exactly friendly. At no point was the conversation heated, but Charlotte read the signs. They wanted him to drop his price. She wanted to stride onto the roundabout and take over negotiations.

Behave. This isn't your fight.

But in some ways, it was. Charlotte's sense of right and wrong had got her in trouble from the first year of school. She'd jump in and stand up and protect until she was exhausted and beaten down and sad. It never stopped her though. Sometimes people needed a champion.

As voices rose, snippets made it to Charlotte.

"Too expensive." From Jonas.

"Be community minded." Terrance.

"Family to feed." Darcy. "New baby almost here."

"Not our problem." Jonas.

Charlotte's fingers had closed into tight balls and she forced them open again before the tension pushed her into action.

Darcy closed his notepad and shook his head.

Jonas stormed off, straight to Sid. They turned away from the roundabout in agitated conversation, but it was too far for Charlotte to hear. Darcy's shoulders had slumped. Her heart went out to him. What a difficult situation, when you need to sell but can't afford to take a big hit on the price.

She narrowed her eyes as she looked back at the corner. Sid and Jonas had turned around again to look at Darcy. They still muttered to each other, but their body language gave away some agreement. Then, Sid patted Jonas' shoulder.

Darcy straightened when Jonas returned to the roundabout. This time, Jonas held out his hand to shake and after a hesitant moment, Darcy took it.

Sid was gone. Charlotte had no idea where he went but he'd virtually melted into the dark. No sign of his car. Jonas and Terrance climbed into their respective cars and drove off in different directions, leaving Darcy to do another measure. Charlotte emerged from her spot.

"Hi, Darcy." She crossed the road and he looked up with surprise that turned into a smile.

"Didn't see you there. How's the tree?"

"Enjoying a bit of shade and lots of sun and water. I think it might just grow up."

"Sorry you paid for it."

"Are you kidding? I'm a sucker for turning broken into whole." Charlotte said. "Are you replacing the tree here?"

Utter relief crossed his face and he nodded. "After a bit of negotiation, yes. I understand the council isn't made of money, but nor am I. For a job this big I must hire someone to help fell the tree, help with transport, and then erect it safely here."

"Where they trying to get a big discount?"

"Apparently I should have donated it. And then they offered quarter what my cost will be."

"But they changed their minds?"

"Still not full price, but I'll make a little bit." Darcy tossed the tape measure and notepad into his car. "Much as it pains us to hear about the break-ins recently, I'm mighty thankful people have chosen to replace their trees with one of ours."

Charlotte smiled. "I imagine children aren't the cheapest people to live with."

He laughed; his face happier than she'd seen all night. "We get there. Just hoping to make enough to cover the outstanding rates on the farm, and then enough for some new wood turning tools. Trained as a carpenter and figured I might start making furniture from some of the trees we sell."

"Nothing like locally made furniture. I'd buy it. Maybe people could return their used trees for recycling?"

Darcy's eyes lit up. "Never thought of that. I could keep a bit aside from each sale and give them something when they come back."

"Or add a little extra and keep that."

"Are you a business manager? I could use someone, for sure."

"Nope. But I have a head full of ideas which are generally quite useless, so don't expect the next gem to be valuable. Goodnight." Charlotte grinned and stepped off the roundabout.

"Night."

Darcy tooted as he passed her a couple of minutes later and she waved. There was no way Darcy was involved in any wrongdoing. He had plans. They were hard working, good people with good values.

Only one thing made her wonder. He'd mentioned council rates. Outstanding ones. If the Christmas Tree farm was under threat of repossession, it might be enough to drive a person to make bad decisions. Sometimes the risk might seem worth it.

CHAPTER TWENTY

THE VIEW FROM THE LOOKOUT AT DAWN WAS WORTH THE CLIMB. After a night of restless sleep, Charlotte decided to burn off the excess energy by retracing her steps from the other night. It was just light enough to avoid needing a flashlight when she'd followed the path from the main road, and the higher she got, the brighter the sky.

Around her, the air was alive with birdsong, competing against the cascade of the falls. It was a bit unnerving to discover how close she'd been at times to slippery edges and possibly falling by wandering around in the dark. Even though the lookout had a sturdy rail, it didn't fully surround the area and a person might lose sight of the edge and tumble over.

And it was a long way down. Charlotte peered over the side. There was an almost sheer drop to the river of at least a hundred metres.

Rosie had mentioned people falling. Charlotte grimaced. Had anyone survived? Perhaps the railing wasn't there when it happened.

Enough of this doom and gloom. It was going to be a glorious day from the appearance of the rapidly lightening sky with its drifts of golden and pink cloud.

Charlotte took the steps down to the bottom of the falls,

conscious of some slippery parts that weren't maintained. The ramp that Rosie mentioned was a mess, full of potholes and overgrown in many places. No wheelchair or pram could safely navigate it. Surely council was responsible for this? Or maybe it was Parks and Wildlife. Easy enough to check later and make a complaint to the right place.

The falls disappeared from view as the steps wound through old forest. Massive ferns and a canopy of ghost gums cooled the air. Charlotte stood still for a moment as a large bird crossed ahead. Its huge red bill and head shield made for a ferocious first impression, but the glossy black top half of the body and brilliant blue bottom belonged to the quite benign Swamp Hen, which Charlotte had seen around the edge of town before. It wandered back to the undergrowth and Charlotte continued.

The path suddenly took a sharp turn and the canopy disappeared. Charlotte stepped onto lush grass at the edge of the large pool at the bottom of the waterfall. The water was clear to the bottom and flowed away slowly to become part of the river. She squatted and trailed her fingers in water that was surprisingly cold. The sheer beauty of the landscape tip-toed into her heart. This really was a place she could love and call home

———

Almost every customer wanted to talk about the meeting last night and what they dubbed the 'Christmas Tree Thief' affair. Some people were outraged that the Forest family were being targeted, but others shared their concerns.

"It does have some fact behind it." One woman looked over her shoulder as she loudly whispered. "That farm has never recovered from the scandal. Apples don't fall far from trees, mark my words!"

"I'll mark your words as utter rubbish." Rosie had muttered the minute the customer left. "With a cherry on top."

Charlotte giggled.

Rosie stared at her so solemnly that Charlotte stopped. "Sorry."

"This is not a laughing matter."

"No. But you are so sweet and always polite to the nth degree so…"

"If you knew what I think sometimes, you'd be whipping out those psychoanalyst tools and measuring me for a straitjacket."

"Nah. Nothing going on with you that needs as much as a sedative. By scandal, did she mean the divorce?" Charlotte tidied rows of Christmas cards on a spinning stand. "How long ago was it?"

"Ten years or so. Darcy had just left home to do an apprenticeship in Geelong."

"Carpentry. He told me last night."

"Okay, you need to explain."

"I will but finish first." Charlotte shuffled some overstocked cards into empty slots.

"Well, it was all very sudden. Darcy's father came to see me, all upset. Wanted to return a book he'd bought for his wife's birthday a couple of days earlier. I gave him a refund and he told me to keep the money. He just didn't want the book because she'd packed up, on her birthday mind you, and told him she was leaving with Octavia's husband. Don't think he ever saw her again."

"Wow. How heartbreaking."

"He was shattered. Let the farm go. Once it was the destination place to buy trees and was a thriving little wholesale nursery. There's greenhouses up there and he sold seedlings and young trees to the garden centres."

"Like the one owned by Veronica?"

"Yes." Rosie wheeled across to Charlotte. "After a year or so, he'd closed the nursery side of it and every Christmas sold less and less. He wasn't well liked by then with his temper, so people went elsewhere."

"Darcy mentioned he has to pay off land rates."

"Did he now? Guess his father left him more than just an underperforming business." Rosie handed Charlotte some money. "Get us some coffees? Then you can tell me why you suddenly know so much about Darcy Forest."

———

When Rosie went for a short lunch break later, Charlotte opened a local region book she'd seen earlier to read up on the Swamp Hen she'd seen on her walk earlier and was pleased she'd identified it correctly. She rather liked birds and might have to buy some binoculars and take bird watching a bit more seriously.

"Interested in our natural wonders, dear?"

Charlotte jumped. She'd not heard Glenys enter the shop and was a bit shocked to find her standing only a few feet away, leaning on a walking stick.

"Glenys. Apologies, I didn't hear you come in."

Glenys tilted her head to one side with a slight smile. "You had your head buried in that book. Do you know, I took some of the photographs in it?"

"You did? Oh, please show me."

For a few minutes, Glenys went through the book showing off her skills, which were excellent. She explained she'd been a wedding photographer for a long time but longed to be known as a wildlife expert.

"I'm so impressed, Glenys. What an interesting life you've led." Finally, Charlotte was able to close the book and slide it back on the shelf. "Is there something in particular you're looking for today?"

"Not as such." Glenys hobbled to the counter and Charlotte went to the opposite side.

"Are you alright? I've not seen you with a walking stick before."

"Oh, it's an old injury that plays up now and then when I overdo things. The thing is, I said some unkind words about the Forest family the other day and wanted to let you and dear Rosie know I was simply out of sorts. In a bit of pain and wasn't being very nice."

"We really didn't notice." Charlotte lied.

"You are too nice. Which is why Rosie has you here. You know all the right things to say which is why the other ladies are surprised you're working in a shop." She leaned toward Charlotte with a conspiring wink. "They think you have a past."

Dread clutched Charlotte's stomach.

"A past? Everyone has one."

"Talk is that you *know* people."

A little bit of the panic subsided.

"Any particular people?"

"Yes." Glenys was so far across the counter she might fall if one palm wasn't on the timber top. "The rich and famous. We think you might have been one of those consultants, or publicists, the ones who tell them what to say and how to say it."

Charlotte managed to keep a straight face. She leaned a bit closer to Glenys. "Well, I can tell you —"

"Hello, Glenys. Back again?" Rosie arrived with a box on her lap.

Glenys straightened, annoyance flashing across her face. "Rosie. Nice to see you."

Even Rosie picked up this wasn't true, but she just raised her eyebrows and moved around to her spot behind the counter. She placed the box on the counter and Glenys immediately looked at it.

"Are you buying another book for the giving box?" Rosie asked. "Everyone is being so generous."

"No. Not today. I have a doctor's appointment so will take my leave." She shuffled off, using her walking stick until she was almost past the window, then picked up her pace without it.

Charlotte groaned and leaned against the counter. "May I lock the door when you aren't here? Please?"

"And what was that all about?"

"She and the 'ladies' have decided I am some kind of past consultant for, as she says, the rich and famous."

"You could go with that. Come up with some fancy stories and have them eating out of your hand. Think of all the sales you'd make."

"You want me to lie? Just to make money?" Charlotte grinned. "What's in the box?"

"This is a present for Trev."

Charlotte's heart did a silly little jump.

"Oh. Will it reach him in time?"

"I hope he might make it up in the next few days. He normally visits, depending of course on what antics that town of his is up to."

Rosie laughed. "As you well know, he can't turn his back when somebody needs him."

"This is true. He's pretty good at fixing things."

That was an understatement. When Charlotte was being held in a cave by a former patient, Trev risked his life propelling down a cliff despite his fear of heights. He wasn't the only person out to catch the man but seeing Trev's face when all seemed lost was a moment she'd never forget.

"Charlie?"

"Oh, sorry. So, is it chocolates?"

"No. Actually, I am still of two minds. Would you give me your opinion?"

"Sure. Not that I know him well enough to be a good judge."

Rosie gave her one of those looks she was getting familiar with. A touch of disbelief and a smattering of 'get real'.

Nestled amongst tissue paper was a photo frame made of timber. The photo was at a sportsground. Three people had their arms around each other, and it took a moment for Charlotte to work it out. Rosie, a man who must be her husband, and Trev as a teenager. He wore cricket gear and held a trophy.

"When was this taken?"

"Trev's team had won the Grand Final for the region and he was named Best and Fairest. That's his dad, my Graeme. He coached the team, so it was double celebrations." Rosie traced Graeme's image with a finger. "I used to go to every game. Take the lunches and do the scoring. Such lovely memories."

"Why are you of two minds? It is a beautiful photograph." Charlotte sat next to Rosie.

"This was the last game Trev played. He was all set to play the following season, and Graeme was coach again, but then I had my accident..."

Charlotte took Rosie's hand. "So, it changed all your lives. And you're worried Trev might feel some regret or relive the fears he would have experienced."

Rosie nodded. There were tears in her eyes and her lips trembled.

"I can understand you might worry about his reaction, but seeing as you asked for my opinion, I'm going to give it to you." Charlotte passed a box of tissues to Rosie with her spare hand. "This photograph captures an important and wonderful moment in time. Whatever happened afterwards is unrelated to the excitement and pride I can see in all three of these faces. This celebrates not only the win, but a family who support and love one another. And now I might take a tissue if you don't mind." Her voice squeaked uncharacteristically.

Rosie passed them back and Charlotte dabbed her eyes. As a psychiatrist, she'd heard many stories of loss and regret, but knew how to file them into her collection of mental boxes to avoid the powerful emotions of her patients. This was different. She had no box set up to lock away this kind of reaction. One borne from caring about the subjects.

She sipped some water as Rosie replaced the cover of the box.

"Good. That's settled then. Would you wrap it for me, please?" Rosie didn't look at Charlotte and there was a tell-tale quiver in her voice.

"I will. So, go and freshen up before the book club ladies arrive and get all judgemental."

With a startled glance out of the window, Rosie wheeled off toward the bathroom. "They'd better not start!"

There was no sight of them, but it got Rosie moving and gave Charlotte a moment to blow her nose and pull herself together. Hopefully, Trev wouldn't react this way. Not that she'd be around when he opened it. Or probably even see him.

CHAPTER TWENTY-ONE

ALL AFTERNOON THE SHOP WAS BURSTING WITH CUSTOMERS, SOME panic buying with Christmas Eve looming. There was no time for anything other than a quick sip of water anytime Charlotte made it to the counter, which was mostly to drop off armfuls of books for Rosie to put through the register.

There was a backlog of books to be gift wrapped, and Charlotte had offered to finish this after the doors closed so the new owners could collect them tomorrow. Rosie was exhausted and when things began to quiet down at about five, Charlotte made her go.

"Because if you insist on staying, I'm going to drive you home, and you have no idea what kind of driver I am." She'd threatened.

"How bad could it be between here and my place?" Rosie was collecting her bag as she talked. "Unless you are like Sid."

"How rude!" Charlotte chuckled. "I can drive much faster."

"Very well, I shall go. I need to shop so appreciate the extra time, darling. I feel bad leaving you to finish gift wrapping."

"No need. I shall close and then wrap, perhaps with a glass of wine. I want to add those last-minute gift ideas to the Facebook page, so can sit down here and upload photos."

A family hurried in, the mother with a look of desperation Charlotte was getting used to seeing. She shooed Rosie out and looked after them. Their arrival was followed by a series of late shoppers and the next half hour flew by.

With a small sigh of relief, Charlotte closed and locked the front door. She turned off all the lights except the one above the counter and counted the takings. Once they were in the safe, she did a quick sweep and tidied up the shop ready for the morning. From upstairs she collected a glass of red wine and returned to the counter, ready to wrap the remaining books.

A tap on the door surprised her and she waved and shook her head as if to say 'closed'. But it was Esther, who mouthed something Charlotte couldn't hear.

Charlotte opened the door a crack. "Hello, I'm sorry but I've closed the registers."

"Oh, I was going home and saw the light. Not buying, just hoped to have a word."

"Come in. But I'll lock you in with me."

Esther slid inside and waited at the counter as Charlotte closed and relocked the door. Her face was the most relaxed Charlotte had seen so far.

She smiled. "I won't hold you up, Charlotte. We sent the photos to the insurance company and they've said they'd like you to provide a brief statement, if you don't mind. They were very nice on the phone, and I got the impression they'll help us."

"Oh, wonderful! Yes, let them have my email address and I can fill in their form or whatever they need. Have the police let you know anything?"

"Sid? He doesn't care. Don't let his car chase through town fool you for a minute because it was all for show." Esther turned red; her hands balled at her side. "There's something going on and us traders? We're all caught in the middle of it."

"I'm listening."

"Council wants us to contribute to a new tree for the roundabout. We already paid for one mid-year when Jonas came around crying poor."

"I heard about them asking for money now, but if you've already paid once it seems unfair. Would you like to sit?"

"No. I really have to get going and I'm sorry to get all upset. We'd all really like some proper policing." She glanced at where Rosie usually worked. "I'm sure we'd all be happy if Trevor was in charge."

"I think he's pretty happy in River's End." Charlotte wished someone would tell her exactly why he wasn't here in Kingfisher Falls.

"I know. He always tells Doug and me he loves it there. But we need good policing and instead we have Sid Browne." Esther headed for the door. "Perhaps he'll come back now you're here."

"Trev? Me? No, it's nothing like that. Here, let me get the lock, it tends to be a bit stiff to turn." Charlotte opened the door and stepped out into the late afternoon sunshine. "I was so pleased to hear Doug say what he did last night."

"He is one for telling things as they are. Both of us are angry anyone would even consider Darcy to be behind all the thefts. I've known him since he was born and there's nothing in him but a good heart and kind spirit."

Back inside, Charlotte took a sip of wine before beginning to wrap. Why did Esther believe she and Trev had something going on? Rosie knew better, although she did worry about her son's love life, or lack thereof, so it probably wasn't coming from her. Maybe just a typical small-town response. People like to gossip. Pity there was nothing to gossip about when it came to Trevor Sibbritt.

———

The wine glass was long empty by the time there was a row of beautifully wrapped books lining the top of the back counter. Charlotte was pleased with herself. As with decorating Christmas trees, she had little experience with gift wrapping, but once Rosie showed her a few tricks, she enjoyed doing it. Using her hands to create something pretty was surprisingly satisfying.

She took a couple of photos of the newly made display near the children's section. It was filled with colourful picture books right up to young adult novels, all discounted until close of business on Christmas Eve. These she uploaded to Facebook, adding a catchy description.

The page had grown again, and there were new reviews. Charlotte couldn't help smiling as she recognised some names who left glowing comments. But then the smile faded. Someone called 'Disenworb the Great' had given one star. Fine, but the words below chilled Charlotte.

Overpriced. Rude staff. Don't shop there.

"What? Rude? Us?" Charlotte heard the shock in her voice and took a deep breath. This was someone having a go. Possibly a competitor. Her mind flew back to the Santa from the next town, happily encouraging the folk of Kingfisher Falls to take their business to his store. Her fingers hovered above the keyboard to respond. Instead, she exited Facebook, and turned off the computer.

Any response needed to be cleverly worded to take the sting out of the review. But not to engage with someone who had an axe to grind. She'd think it over and speak to Rosie in the morning.

Last of the lights off, Charlotte rattled the front door to be certain it was locked. Sid's police car drove past, ever so slowly, then he did a U-turn. She wasn't about to speak to him today, not after hours and in a dark shop, so Charlotte retreated behind a bookcase, where she hoped she couldn't be seen from the street.

He parked outside and climbed out. Sid wasn't in a hurry. He lit a cigarette and leaned against his bonnet as he smoked, staring into the shop. Charlotte's senses were on high alert. He tossed the still-smoking butt onto the pavement and wandered along the shopfront. For a moment he looked through the window with the Christmas tree, then took out a phone and possibly took a photo. She was too far away to be certain.

The phone returned to his pocket and he moved along the windows to the door, turning the handle then pushing on it until it creaked. Charlotte's heart raced and she clenched her hands to keep herself still. What the hell was he up to?

At the other window he put both hands against it and peered in.

His eyes seemed to be directly on Charlotte, and she held her breath. This was not normal behaviour for a police officer. Esther was right. Something was wrong in this town and it included at least some shire councillors and the only police officer in the area. A couple wandered past taking their dog for a walk and nodded to him. He nodded back. The minute they were gone, he shot back to his car and slid in.

Charlotte waited until his car was gone and then she sped out of the shop, double checking she'd locked the back door, and up her stairs. She locked the door and pulled the chain across, something she didn't normally worry about.

From the balcony she looked for his car. He'd gone. At least out of sight.

CHAPTER TWENTY-TWO

TOO TIRED AND DISTRACTED TO COOK, CHARLOTTE WANDERED across to Italia in the hope she'd get a table without a booking. The other night from her table at the Indian restaurant across the road, she'd seen how busy this one was.

Tonight, it was almost deserted, and she was whisked to a round table with a bright tablecloth near a window. Although there were few patrons, the kitchen was noisy and several delivery drivers with 'Italia to Home' on their tops waited for their bags to be packed. Behind the pass, Doug called orders and cut pizzas.

"Welcome to Italia. I'm Bronnie and will look after you this evening." A friendly faced older woman, red hair pulled back in a bun, appeared tableside with a menu and notepad. "Would you like to order a drink first?"

"Hello, Bronnie. I'm Charlotte. Um, yes, maybe a glass of red wine."

"We have some nice Chianti if you wish?"

"I'd like that."

When Bronnie returned with her wine, Charlotte ordered pumpkin gnocchi, suddenly ravenous and longing for a nice meal. She was no kind of cook, not really. From a young age she'd been responsible for feeding herself and often her mother and taught herself some basics. Enough to get by.

The months she lived at Palmerston House made a difference, with Elizabeth happy to let her help with meals and teaching her little tricks. Such as knowing when fish was cooked properly, and how to make delicious wedges in the oven rather than frying them. It didn't interest her enough to make her take lessons, but at least now she had more than the standard five or six meals she'd rotated for years.

What did interest Charlotte was people watching. Humans were such intriguing things. She missed her practice at times. Missed some of the patients she'd helped.

An elderly couple were shown to a table and then a young family to another. The couple smiled at the children and then at each, holding hands over the table. They reminded her of Thomas and Martha Blake from River's End. They were a couple with stories to tell, and such love for each other.

"Here we are. The gnocchi is steaming hot so please give it a minute." Bronnie set a large bowl in front of Charlotte.

"This smells lovely! Bronnie, I'm surprised it isn't any busier. Or is this a weekday thing?"

Bronnie frowned. "No, this is a Christmas tree thief thing, I'm afraid. People don't want to leave their houses in case they are next. Takeaway is busy, but not the restaurant. I sent home all the other waiting staff early."

Charlotte savoured a mouthful of the wine as Bronnie went to collect menus for the other tables.

The whole town was being hurt by the people behind the thefts. Was this their objective? To frighten families and the shopkeepers for some reason?

"But why?" she murmured. "Who is benefitting?"

Sid came to mind immediately, but this was baffling because all he'd got out of it was criticism for the car chase. Maybe it was just some bored thugs with nothing better to do.

The gnocchi melted in Charlotte's mouth. She took time to enjoy the meal and atmosphere. Doug noticed her and waved.

Deciding she was too full for dessert, Charlotte paid and thanked Bronnie for a lovely meal and service. The air was warm and there were people walking along the main street, so she went window shopping. She wanted to find something to give Rosie for Christmas and so far, had little in the way of ideas.

A couple of shops caught her interest. The first was a homeware shop. Its window was brightly lit to display shelf upon shelf of Christmas ideas. Dinner sets, vases, glassware, beautiful tea towels and lined, thick towels, and all kinds of knick-knacks. There was a row of ceramic teapots and these appealed to Charlotte. Rosie drank coffee at work but had mentioned her morning cup of tea more than once. She filed that idea away for later.

Esther's dress shop was more than simply clothing. She sold shoes, belts, wraps, hats, and scarves.

The scarves were all lightweight for summer, cotton or silk, and in a range of patterns and colours from pastels to bold. Charlotte particularly liked one with a soft green background and a vibrant dash of emerald. It said 'Rosie' all over.

Happy with her finds, Charlotte crossed the road. There were less people about now and she found herself walking faster than normal.

You're braver than this.

She deliberately slowed her steps, enjoying the walk in the evening air. The corner was ahead and once she went over the side street, the bookshop was only a little bit further. There were some people looking in its window.

Charlotte didn't want to disturb them so stepped onto the grass verge. She glanced at the window. Their faces were reflected in the glass.

Their...what?

She stopped abruptly. Two men, both with longish dark hair. But where their faces should be...it didn't make sense. They were misshapen. Her brain struggled to frame what her eyes saw. They turned.

Masks. Nothing more than scary Halloween masks.

Neither man moved.

And Charlotte couldn't. Her legs were frozen in place. Her mouth opened but nothing came out.

One man stepped her way and she instinctively backed off the grass verge onto the road as a car approached.

The other man grabbed the first man's arm. "Leave it, Darro."

They took off away from the bookshop, pulling off their masks as they ran.

"Wait!" Charlotte found her voice and her legs and sprinted after them. "Come back. I need to ask you questions."

They disappeared around a corner and she halted, panting. What on earth was she doing chasing them? The car that had scared them off pulled up alongside and a window wound down.

"Are you okay?" It was a young woman. "Do you need a lift?"

"No. I mean, yes, I'm fine thanks. I live here."

"If you're sure." The car left before Charlotte could ask what they saw. If they'd seen the masks, then she had witnesses.

To what? Charlotte hurried upstairs and locked herself in. She should be calling the police. But she knew what would happen. Sid Browne would come calling and make sure her concerns didn't make it past him. She wasn't about to have that man anywhere near her.

Somehow, she had to find Darro and his friend and discover what was going on. And she had to do it on her own. Rosie didn't need to be frightened.

CHAPTER TWENTY-THREE

GREY SKIES AND STEADY RAIN GREETED CHARLOTTE WHEN SHE finally woke. Dreams had filled her night. People staring at her through the bookshop window. Just staring. And then a dream that had reoccurred her whole life and always woke her in frozen fear, when a simple walk along a street turned to nightmare as lights went off and breathing behind her closed in.

She'd not had that particular dream for a while and it unnerved Charlotte. It came when she struggled with controlling her environment and was a reminder to take a step back. Except she couldn't. Not from the sinister behaviour of too many people in this town.

With a stronger than normal coffee, Charlotte checked on the tree on the balcony. It was one little thing that made her happy, seeing it recover a bit more each day. She was sure it was growing now, the tips of its branches green and healthy.

"One day, I'll find the perfect place and plant you. Would you like that?"

Now she was talking to trees. It made sense though. She always told her patients to verbalise their fears and worries, or at least write them down. Instead of keeping them in an endless cycle of increasing concern, this was a simple and effective way to manage them.

"Doctor heal thyself. Okay, tree, I have a problem." She sipped coffee for a while. The rain was slowing. Humid air promised more rain or a storm.

"I think someone is trying to scare me. Or Rosie." Time to have some tree-therapy. "Sid was very interested in the bookshop last night, then our thieves—alleged or not—did the same. But you may have noticed they went a step further and used masks."

The tree moved a little as a breeze picked up.

"Absolutely. I agree they might have used them to protect their identity. But why were they even there? Did someone know I was heading back?"

A shiver ran up her spine. If she was being watched, why? Was Sid so determined to uncover her past that he'd stoop to this? She'd need to leave Kingfisher Falls. Charlotte's fingers reached for the bracelet. Was there no place she could be free of the bad decisions she'd made and have a chance to start over?

Before the panic swept through her body, Charlotte stood. There was no reason to believe Sid was doing more than bluffing. Intimidating a woman who'd stood up to him. Whatever was going on in town was not of her doing, nor would she stand by and let good people be hurt. She should call Trev. Ask him some hypothetical questions.

He'll drop everything to get here and fix it.

She sighed. This was a new predicament. Not being able to speak to police about crimes, scare tactics, and goodness knows what else. When the only police officer in town was in the middle of it, what was she to do? Rosie's call to the general police line wasn't exactly taken seriously, or if it was, had been explained away by Sid. And Trev had no jurisdiction here, just a mother he'd needlessly worry about if Charlotte said anything.

Today, she'd take control. No more frightening dreams if she faced things head on.

———

"You do look so tired, darling." Rosie peered over the top of her glasses as Charlotte set down two takeaway coffees on the counter. "I feel terrible putting you through so much."

"I love it. The customers are fun, and I enjoy making everything look nice. Even sweeping out the front makes me feel like I...well, belong here."

"Well, you do belong here and I, for one, am very happy to know you."

Not if you really knew me.

Charlotte felt her lips tighten and tried to smile, managing a small one. She needed to fulfil her earlier resolve. Face the fears, deal with the problems.

"But we are almost there. Apart from today, we only have three shopping days. I had considered opening on Sunday, but we both need time to prepare for our own Christmas day, don't we?" Rosie's smile held a question.

"If you still would like me to come for Christmas—"

"Yes! Oh, goodie! The cats will be delighted." Rosie clapped her hands. "The forecast is for a hot day, so let's make it dinner?"

"The cats? Sure, I'm hoping they know how to cook?"

"Funny."

"What shall I bring?"

"Nothing."

"Not happening. Let me know by Sunday and I'll go shopping."

Customers came in, taking Rosie's attention. Charlotte told her stomach to stop doing silly flutters. Christmas dinner with a person she liked so much was nothing to be anxious about. And now she had an even better gift idea. There must be somewhere around here that sold pet toys.

———

"Not as such," Esther folded the emerald scarf into a box. "I think the garden centre carries a small range of pet supplies, otherwise you'd need to go to Gisborne. There's a lovely shop there."

"I can't go too far until I get my windscreen repaired. Is the garden centre walking distance?"

"Yes, I'll draw you a map. But there's a mobile windscreen company in town."

"Is it Ivan?"

"Yes. Did you try him?"

"I'd forgotten Rosie gave me his number." Charlotte said.

"Call him today. I was talking to Ivan the other day and he mentioned the family is heading off to their beach house for Christmas."

Esther drew a little map. "Here you go. About ten minutes each way. Veronica is apparently keeping it open until seven each night this week so you could easily make it after work. I imagine the book-shop is crazy busy."

"It is. And I feel a bit guilty leaving Rosie alone but have no gifts at all yet."

With a laugh, Esther handed over the box. "Rosie is a power-house. She can manage a store full of customers and take in a delivery at the same time. Probably unpack it as well. But I am thrilled she has you there. With Braden leaving to go to the city, we did wonder if she'd simply keep going on her own or sell up."

"I'm learning so much from her."

"From what I hear, you are an asset. How lucky was Rosie to find someone with such a lot of retail experience?"

Instead of correcting Esther, Charlotte smiled and took the box. "Thanks for the map. And this. I think Rosie will like it."

On the way back to the bookshop, Charlotte phoned Ivan and was surprised when he said he would come around this afternoon.

The bookshop only had a couple of customers, both chatting to Rosie, so Charlotte dashed upstairs and left the box on the kitchen counter. She found her car keys to move the car onto the driveway, happy the rain had stopped. At least if she was busy when Ivan arrived, he wouldn't need to wait around for her.

Her eyes lingered on the door at the back of the garage. What an interesting find the cane trunk was. If Rosie didn't mind, she'd love to spend some time in there. How wonderful if she could reunite the owner of the contents with it. Something about the wedding dress and teddy bear with the bundle of baby clothes stirred her emotions. There was a story there.

CHAPTER TWENTY-FOUR

MID-AFTERNOON, A VAN PULLED INTO THE DRIVEWAY. THE LOGO across the vehicle—*Kingfisher Falls Windscreens and Glass*—was in bright pink, and Rosie told Charlotte to tend to Ivan.

A big man with a peaked cap, he stepped back from checking her windscreen and offered a large hand. "Afternoon, miss."

"Nice to meet you. I'm Charlotte. Or Charlie. Is it fixable?"

"Sure. No cracks appearing so no need to change the whole thing. Have it done for you in a jiffy. I'll stick my head in when it's done."

True to his word, it was under half an hour later when he wandered in. Charlotte was finishing up with a customer, so he browsed. Rosie was ringing up a sale from him when Charlotte came over.

"Ivan's donating some children's books, Charlie."

"That's so kind."

"Nah." Ivan shuffled his feet. "Got grandkids and would hate to think another kid went without. Be nice if these made their way to little Lachie."

"Lachie Forest?" Charlotte asked.

Ivan nodded. "He's a good kid."

"I met him last week. Rosie, can we make that happen?"

"Why don't we put them to one side." Rosie did so as she spoke. "Charlie will wrap them up and we'll pop his name on them. Someone from the local charity group are dropping by on Saturday to collect what we have, so I'll talk to them."

After Charlotte paid Ivan, she put the car away, relieved to see a clear windscreen. He was at his van, packing up.

"Where'd you pick that stone up?" he asked.

"I was on the road back from the Christmas Tree farm. Went to get a little tree and of all things, got pulled over by Senior Constable Browne."

Ivan gave her a look of disbelief. "Up there? Were you speeding?"

"Hardly. But he wanted to check my licence and while I waited, somebody hooned past and threw up a dust storm, including stones."

"And Sid chased after them?"

Charlotte bit her bottom lip. She didn't know Ivan. He might be Sid's best friend. This was a time for caution. "He didn't see what happened."

"Humph. Didn't care, you mean. You are very polite."

"You don't happen to know who owns a dark blue ute? Not all that modern, but not really old. Sorry, not good with cars."

He chuckled. "Very descriptive. There's a few around. Was that what did the damage?"

"Yeah." Amongst other things.

"Let you know if I think of any." With a tug on the front of his cap, Ivan closed the door and got into the van.

How interesting so many locals had little respect for Sid. It was as though they simply accepted that he was in charge but would do nothing. Charlotte knew if she was in Kingfisher Falls for any length of time, she'd end up reporting him for some reason or other.

"All fixed?" Rosie asked.

"He is great. And how sweet to buy those books."

"We have a lovely community here. At least, for the most part. I've been thinking and wanted to ask your opinion on where we donate the money to. We're getting quite a stash of five dollar notes now!"

Every time someone donated one of the books, Rosie took five dollars from the till and added to a locked metal box under the counter. At the end of each day, it went into the safe.

"Do you have anything in mind?"

"If it was my choice, I'd make sure it found its way to Darcy. Help with those rates."

Charlotte grinned. "I love it. Every bit must help."

"And he's too proud to ask for help. All that family needs is a little bit of breathing space, and Christmas is the perfect time to give them that."

As Charlotte wrapped the books up, a warm glow filled her. Despite the thefts and some shady characters, Kingfisher Falls had a heart of gold.

———

Even though the car was fixed, Charlotte elected to walk to the garden centre. If she purchased anything too large to carry, she'd collect it later. There was no sign of the earlier rain as she followed Esther's map. It took her to the roundabout, then left and along a slightly winding road with houses on large blocks of land, some set back, and all very pretty with Christmas decorations in the gardens.

The garden centre was on a corner. Customers had to walk through the shop first. There was nobody around. A huge pile of boxed, artificial Christmas trees cluttered the entrance with a large 'sale' sign leaning against them.

Open roller doors at the back led to the outdoor area which stretched a long way back. Walkways went off in different directions and there were shade sails over some areas. Charlotte was curious about Veronica after the meeting that night and hoped she'd be able to observe her at work.

She heard her before seeing her. From the back of the property, Veronica's voice screeched in an angry tirade. Charlotte followed the sound. What was noticeable was the lack of stock. A few shrubs here. A handful of roses there. Seedlings left out in the sun were almost dried out. Water gushed down the path from somewhere.

"How many times do I have to tell you the same thing?" Veronica was still yelling as Charlotte reached a large greenhouse.

Veronica, dressed in a short skirt and blouse, faced the other way, where a teenaged girl stood, face as red as her hair.

"I…I'm sorry. But they are almost dried out in here—"

"Are you telling me how to run my own business?" Veronica almost stamped her foot.

Charlotte would have been amused but the poor girl was distraught. This was no way to treat anyone and Charlotte wanted to tell the older woman off. But jumping into an unknown situation was likely to cause more grief than remedy it. She coughed.

Two sets of eyes spun to Charlotte. The girl's expression was thankful, but Veronica's face might have been carved from ice.

"Hi. Just looking for some gift ideas." Charlotte made her voice friendly, as though she'd seen nothing out of the ordinary.

Veronica shook her fingers at the girl. "Leave for the day. Go."

The girl flew past Charlotte, head down. Her heart went out for the youngster and the friendliness dropped from her voice. "Your daughter?"

"Staff. Stupid girl has no idea what she's doing."

Screaming at her reflects on you. Not her. Poor kid.

"You work in the bookshop. You're the new hope for Rose."

"New hope? I don't understand."

Veronica picked up the end of a running hose. She pointed it into a half-empty raised pond. "I need to turn this off." She stalked off and Charlotte followed.

"What does new hope mean?"

"Poor old Rose can't keep going forever now, can she? Dragging herself from home to work and back again. One wonders what the state of her house is because I'm certain she doesn't get any help." She leaned through bushes to find the tap.

It took all of Charlotte's self-control not to push Veronica completely into the bushes. She practiced deep breathing until the other woman straightened.

"Oh, you've not been to her lovely home? You could eat off the floor there. And so welcoming." Charlotte gazed at a pile of old pots. "Just like the bookshop. As neat as a pin."

Veronica followed her gaze and her face hardened. "If Rose's doing so well, why does she need you?"

"Anyway, I did mention I came to look for Christmas gifts, but you don't have very much?"

"We've been busy. Too busy to order, in fact. What do you want?"

"Cat toys. And perhaps something for the garden. A windchime?"

Play nice, Charlie. Works better that way.

With a dramatic sigh, Veronica was on the move again, this time toward the building. "I only have a small selection of things for pets. Not an animal lover so once they're gone, they're gone. But there might be some windchimes somewhere up here."

Charlotte stopped to smell a tiny pot with a lovely white rose. Such an evocative perfume. Her hand hovered, ready to collect the pot, but she couldn't keep collecting plants until she'd worked out what was already in the small garden behind the shop. She'd offered to maintain it and Rosie had been thrilled.

A moment later she stepped into the building and looked around. Veronica was behind a counter, reading something on her phone. She pointed to a corner without lifting her head. By now, Charlotte had no intention of giving this woman a cent, not even if she found the best gift ever.

It took less than five minutes of rummaging through a box on a shelf to find that what might have once been nice cat toys were all damp and falling apart.

Along a wall were sealed boxes. Across them, in black pen, were words such as 'saucepans', 'glassware', 'shoes', 'hats', and 'books'. Books?

Charlotte didn't bother searching for windchimes.

As she made for the door, Veronica suddenly looked up. "Nothing? I've been waiting and nothing?"

"Nothing. I've been looking and...well, I remembered a friend of mine can make a windchime to order. But thanks."

Hands on hips, the fury on the other woman's face was scary. Well, it would be for a teenager, so no wonder the poor girl had run. Surely there'd be better jobs around town?

Outside, Charlotte breathed deeply of the slightly cooler air. There were a few drops of rain and she was ready to go home via a supermarket. And she was going to ask Darcy if he'd make her a wind chime from his own timber once he had time. Something made with love and sold by an ethical person.

CHAPTER TWENTY-FIVE

SHOPPING WAS EASIER THIS TIME AND CHARLOTTE ARRIVED HOME with two bags of fresh produce and other necessities. She opened the laptop as dinner cooked and reread the email from Lakeview Care.

If her mother was suffering as much as Maggie implied, why had they not brought in another specialist and got another opinion? New medication wasn't always the answer. Angelica Dean was a tough lady, despite her many mental health issues. Charlotte had always believed quality counselling, coupled with the right combination of medication, was key to giving her mother the most comfortable life.

As Angelica's carer for a while, she'd had success with this approach. For one wonderful year, she'd had her mother. And Angelica was amazing. Smart, funny in ways Charlotte never expected, and at times, deep compassion and regret for the life she'd forced on her child.

No childhood. No teenage years. Just seven years old to adult in one moment when Dad left for the last time.

Thanks Mum. Thanks Dad.

Charlotte closed her eyes and regulated her breathing, forcing out the negative until she could stop her hands shaking. Being reactive wasn't a long-term strategy and she needed to be the grown-up in all of this.

After checking dinner wasn't burning, she dialled Queensland.

"Lakeview Care, Maggie speaking."

"Maggie, this is Charlotte Dean. I'm sorry to take a couple of days to call."

"Dr Dean, thank you. I thought perhaps I had the wrong details for you. Did you receive the parcel we sent?"

"Oh. Yes, the box. I'm not certain what to do with Mum's things. But if you're sure she doesn't want them?" Charlotte glanced in the direction of the bedroom where she'd left the box behind a closed door. "I haven't gone through it yet."

"Angelica really hadn't touched anything in months." Maggie said. "She's retreating into herself. Doesn't want to be involved with any of the activities she used to enjoy. Nor be part of any outings."

"Is she doing regular counselling sessions?"

"No. Part of the problem began when there were some staff changes. Angelica hasn't taken to the new psychiatrist and we can't really force her to see him."

Charlotte shook her head. "Find a female. There are sufficient funds to cover private consultations." Irritation swept through her. "You must remember we went through something similar a few years ago with a male therapist. Shall I find someone?"

Maggie's voice was hesitant. "No. No, I'm happy to do so, but... well, I think it is more this time."

"Let's take one step at a time. If you can arrange a consult with a suitably qualified female psychiatrist and see if she has ideas about Mum's status. And how long since she's had a full physical?"

"She's due." Maggie sounded more positive. "I'll arrange both and let you know once I have some news."

A few minutes later, Charlotte hung up. Lakeview Care was a caring, professional place but sometimes they overlooked simple factors. Mum never liked having men around, not since Dad left.

This was a good step. Charlotte was far from ready to visit, but this communication helped more than she'd expected. One step at a time. For her as well as her mother.

———

Charlotte ate dinner out on the balcony by candlelight. She had plans for the area now she was using it so often. New paint for a start. The balcony was simply an extension of the apartment, with one side a full brick wall, two sides open apart from the railings, and the glass sliding doors and window to back inside. The brick was painted grey, peeling and uninviting.

The floor was just as bad. Unsealed concrete had seen much better days. And even the railings were overdue for new paint and some brightening up. Charlotte finished the last of her pasta bake and pushed the plate aside.

After Christmas, the bookshop was closed until the first week of January. She'd check with Rosie first, but assuming she didn't mind some improvements, Charlotte might spend some of the time refreshing the balcony. And then she could buy some planters and grow herbs and flowers along the rails where the sun shone most of the day. The windchime would hang in the corner. And her little tree would be fine in its pot until the end of summer.

Behind the shop was a small backyard. Charlotte had only been out there a couple times and not long enough to see what was there apart from a clothesline. She had a little bit of exploring to do once Christmas was past.

Out on the street, a slow-moving heavy vehicle passed the book-shop. A flatbed truck, much bigger than Darcy's, and with a small crane at the back. Trussed and tied to the truck was a massive pine tree. Charlotte leaned over the railing as the truck pulled up close to the roundabout. A police car had blocked off one exit and Sid was tossing witches hats around the truck.

Darcy's tree. Probably made sense to put it up at night when the roads were quieter. Charlotte watched for a while as another man helped Darcy untie the tree, then hook it up to the crane. Sid was out of sight although his patrol car lights still flashed. Just as well the rain had cleared again. Getting the huge tree upright was a big enough job without the weather being against them.

Much as she wanted to wander down and observe the construction, Sid's presence stopped Charlotte.

Charlotte carried her plate inside, locking the door after herself. There was a book that needed finishing and she might as well do it tonight.

———

Sleep came in the early hours, after the last page was devoured. Charlotte adored mysteries and thrillers and this one was riveting. She slid beneath the sheets with a happy sigh and fallen asleep quickly.

She woke early despite the short night. Dawn was barely appearing, yet Charlotte longed to stretch her legs. All this wonderful country air.

Curious to see the new tree, she power-walked to the roundabout and stopped to gaze up at the lovely pine. Not as tall as its predecessor, its dark green foliage filled the space left behind. It was on a metal stand which was attached to the concrete centre of the roundabout by lots of bolts. Short of a chainsaw, nobody was moving this beauty.

"I like this one better."

Charlotte jumped. It was Mr Chen, walking a golden retriever. She couldn't help herself and reached out to stroke the dog's velvet ears.

"Sorry, didn't mean to startle you." He said. "This is Mason."

"Mason is a stunner. He reminds me of a dog I used to know."

"Used to?"

"Oh, he lives in the town I lived in before here. Fit and happy, and enjoying the attention of several families." Randall was Christie and Martin's dog, but he adored almost everyone and was a particular favourite of Thomas.

"Typical goldie. Who do you think is stealing all the trees?"

"Me? I really don't know anyone well enough to guess."

"And I've been here for ten years and can't imagine why this is happening." Mr Chen nodded. "Mystery for sure. Well, we need to get home."

"Nice to see you. Merry Christmas." Charlotte smiled. Really smiled. The words made her ridiculously happy for some reason. Was Christmas behind her new attitude?

"Merry Christmas to you."

Charlotte watched them head up the street and turn the corner. How lovely to meet another goldie here so far away from the town where Randall lived. She missed him. For that matter, she missed River's End.

Her tummy rumbled and she wandered home. Elizabeth would be making Palmerston House into a Christmas wonderland and probably Angus was at her side. If she was a betting person—and she wasn't—she'd expect Martha and Thomas to have Christmas at their cottage and include as many of the townsfolk as would fit. Christie and Martin would spend their first Christmas together as husband and wife.

And Trev. Much as she tried, Charlotte couldn't get the sudden image of him out of her mind. The cheerful smile. Even when he was serious, he never came over as angry or mean. And he looked after himself. No doubt.

Stop that at once.

But she missed his eyes. His kind, understanding eyes.

It was only when she paused to glance into the bookshop window to check everything looked nice that she realised she had wrapped her arms around herself.

CHAPTER TWENTY-SIX

CHARLOTTE HAD NEVER SEEN ROSIE SO BRIGHT AND HAPPY. AND this was a woman who always exuded a calming kind of joy. She'd arrived in before opening, tinsel decorating her wheelchair and wearing a Santa hat. She insisted Charlotte wear one as well.

"Fine, but I'd be better as an elf."

"I will consider that next year." Rosie was halfway to the kitchen and called over her shoulder. "Actually, I won't. Next year you will be the boss."

Charlotte sank onto her stool with a soft thud. Rosie really thought she would be the one. From the moment she'd stepped inside the bookshop—in fact, before that, when she'd seen the beautiful window display—Charlotte was lost in admiration.

Charlotte and Rosie kept in touch after the visit and when things got too hard for her in River's End, Charlotte accepted Rosie's offer of a job and accommodation. She'd fallen in love with the bookshop and from day one harboured a secret hope she'd somehow be good enough to eventually take over.

"Hat on head, young lady!" Rosie wagged her finger at Charlotte with a big smile. "You were miles away."

"I was." Charlotte shoved the hat on and flicked the pom-pom to the back. "I went to the garden centre after work last night."

"Did you now? And was Veronica around?"

"Screaming at her poor staff member near the greenhouse."

Rosie frowned. "Not the young lass who is there on weekends? I imagine she's on holidays from school and can work more."

"She was just about in tears and I'm glad I showed myself before it got any nastier. Who on earth treat someone that way?" Charlotte shook her head before the frustration built up again. "Is it usually low on stock?"

"I haven't been there often, not since Veronica took over. Initially I bought a few plants, but they were always in poor shape and when I accidently took home a disease which went through my vegetables, well, I stopped going there."

"She doesn't like animals." As if that explained everything she disliked about Veronica, Charlotte headed for the front door. "Coffee?"

"Oh, my. And I think some pastries, given that information!"

———

As Charlotte emerged from the café with coffees and a box of goodies, she glanced at the roundabout. Two men worked around it on scaffolding, decorating it with thick streams of tinsel and giant baubles. It was already looking beautiful and other people stopped to watch.

"That new tree is so gorgeous!" she announced as she handed one coffee to Rosie and put her own one behind the counter. "There's pastries and cupcakes in case we need them later."

"I like the way you think." Rosie peeked in the box. "And agree about the tree. From now I think the real ones are the way to go."

"I disagree!"

Octavia stood stiffly just inside the door, hugging her large handbag to her body.

"Good morning. You mentioned that before, Octavia. Why does it worry you so much?" Rosie wheeled herself around the counter.

"Surely artificial trees that are made from non-recyclable material are much less friendly to our planet?"

"If they were all in pots like the one in your window then perhaps, I could agree. But most of them are cut down, and then die. And cutting them down means less oxygen and no place for the kingfishers."

"The kingfishers don't nest in pines. And they make plenty of oxygen as they grow. Anyway, Darcy replants for every tree he takes." Rosie tilted her head at Octavia.

"But so much gets wasted!"

"Darcy is going to build furniture from returned trees." Charlotte added.

Octavia ignored her.

"Rosie, I came to see if those books are here yet."

"The book club reads?" Rosie shook her head. "Not until the delivery in the new year. We discussed this the other day."

Lips pursed, Octavia glared at Rosie.

What was wrong now?

"I see. It was my hope you'd try a bit harder to retain loyal customers, but if the book club is not important, then regrettably, we will purchase our books elsewhere."

Charlotte got to her feet, ready to go around the counter. Rosie's eyes didn't leave Octavia's face, but she shot out her palm at Charlotte. Stay put.

"Octavia, I'm very sorry you feel this way. As I explained, the wholesalers take a break at this time of year so although I've ordered the books, they won't be delivered here until they come back from their holiday. Glenys mentioned the first meeting of the book club could be slightly delayed allowing for the books to arrive and be in the members hands."

"Glenys Lane is not in charge of the book club! I am now the president and things will be done the way I say."

"The order was placed, Octavia."

"Then unplace it. Rosie." Octavia leaned toward Rosie, almost hissing. "Marguerite and I knew you and your son had it in for Sid, but now you've employed Trev's girlfriend you might as well kiss this shop goodbye."

With that, she trounced out.

"He's not my..." Charlotte began but the woman was gone. She turned her attention to Rosie, who hadn't moved. "What was that about?"

"Nothing. Forget it." Rosie stared out the door.

Nothing, my foot.

Charlotte finally came around the counter but now, Rosie was on the move, out of the shop and in the opposite direction Octavia took. Charlotte followed.

"Rosie?"

"Back soon. Need to think."

There were tears in her words and Charlotte wanted to run after her. But customers were heading in and she stood for a moment, torn in two. Rosie needed time. Hands clenched, Charlotte went inside.

———

Charlotte somehow served customer after customer with a smile, although perhaps a bit forced. Her stomach churned every time her thoughts strayed to Octavia's savage words. The woman had never been nice, not in her limited exposure, but the way she'd spoken to Rosie was disgusting.

"There you are, all ready for you to write in the card and put beneath the tree." She handed over a gift-wrapped boxset of books to the last in a series of patient and polite customers.

Glenys came in and straight past the counter with a slight smile at Charlotte. Why was she being nice? Did she not know what had happened?

"How may I assist, Glenys?" With every ounce of civility she could muster, she went to help. "New book?"

"No, dear. Not for me. But I wanted to buy another for the donation box."

"How generous to buy more. Do you have anything in mind?" Charlotte asked.

"Children's books. Well, something for a little boy. Darcy's little boy because I might ask it be given to him, if that is possible?" There was hesitance in her voice. "Without anyone knowing I gave it."

"Of course. There are a few donations for him so I will ensure whatever you select will go straight to him. And anonymously if that's what you really want."

"Thank you. What would you recommend?"

A few minutes later, Glenys had paid and left. Still a bit puzzled by the need for secrecy and apparent friendliness, Charlotte quickly wrapped the book before the next rush.

Where was Rosie? It was more than an hour since she'd left, and her phone was here behind the counter so Charlotte couldn't even call. Had she gone to the lookout? A shard of fear stabbed Charlotte's heart. What if she'd fallen?

The shop had a 'back soon' sign and Charlotte reached for it. Customers could come back. Even if, according to Octavia, there would soon be none.

"No need, Charlie." Rosie was back.

Relief replaced the fear. "Just wanted to see what the door looked like with this on it."

"I'm sorry."

"Where you at the lookout?"

Rosie nodded as she parked the wheelchair behind the counter. "There's something soothing about the falls. Puts things into perspective."

"Agree. I've been there twice now and came away happier each time than I went."

"Has it been busy?" Rosie asked.

"Yes. And some more donations for the giving box. I forgot to take the last five dollars out."

"I'll do it." Rosie opened the register and removed a note. "Anyone we know?"

"Mm."

"Oh, that good. Who?"

"Glenys."

For the first time since arriving back, Rosie looked at Charlotte.

The rims of her eyes were red and a bit swollen. Her skin was pale although she'd been out in the sun on a warm day. There was the slightest tremor in her hand as she transferred the money to the metal box.

"I see."

Charlotte sank next to her. "Would you like to go home? I'm perfectly fine here and you need a chance to...deal with what happened."

Rosie took her hand and squeezed it. "I'm better staying. The little break let me park Octavia's behaviour for the moment and I'd rather be working. Thank you, darling."

"Do you want to talk?"

"Not yet. And not here."

"I'll find us both some water and we can prepare for the next onslaught."

As Charlotte stood, Rosie kept hold of her. "Charlotte. I fear I've involved you in problems not of your making. Just by association you've come under fire."

"I have no time for judgemental people. If the Octavia's and Marguerite's of this world don't like me, I'm not worried."

"Even so, we can't go through life with too many enemies."

"Rosie, you've been so kind to me. Whatever is going on with them, whatever their problems are, we'll deal with them. When you're ready."

With a slight nod, Rosie released her. River's End suddenly felt very uncomplicated compared to the undercurrents and suspicions of the good—and not so good—people of Kingfisher Falls.

CHAPTER TWENTY-SEVEN

CHARLOTTE WALKED HOME WITH ROSIE. THE AFTERNOON HAD been much quieter than the morning, allowing them to catch up on cleaning and restocking. Charlotte had dashed to the bank to deposit the last few days' takings.

There'd been no more talk about Octavia and, Rosie, although quiet, had regained her composure. When she'd asked Charlotte if she'd like to come over to visit the cats and have a drink, there was no hesitation in answering yes.

At the roundabout they stopped to stare at the fully decorated tree. It was a wonderful sight with its dark green foliage and fairy lights just visible in the still bright afternoon sunshine. "This is what a town tree should be!" Charlotte exclaimed.

"Does River's End do this?" Rosie started off again and they crossed the road.

"No idea. I arrived early in the year and left...two weeks ago? A bit more?"

"Oh. For some reason I thought you'd lived there for much longer. So, why did you choose to move there?"

"Kind of a strange story. I'd had a patient in Brisbane who talked about the town a few times. He was the one who thought he was the rightful heir to Palmerston House."

Rosie glanced up with her lips open in surprise. "I know some of this story but what made you want to live there? Did he describe it as somewhere particularly inviting?"

"He'd never been. And I'd had no conscious plan to end up living there."

No. You just ran away from everything and headed south with nothing but a suitcase.

"I don't mean to pry, darling."

A couple approached them walking their dog and said hello to Rosie by name as they passed. The moment gave her a chance to find the right words.

"You can ask me anything, Rosie. Really, anything at all. I just can't always answer well because there's stuff in…well, my past, and around work and…it is complicated. About River's End? I left a bad situation in Queensland and drove where the road took me. When I found myself in Victoria, something made me look up Palmerston House and I discovered it was a bed and breakfast near the sea. Sounded perfect."

More people passed. Families. Older couples, hand in hand. "Good to see people feeling a bit more secure again." Rosie commented. "I hope whoever was stealing those trees has given up, or left town. Preferably gone for good."

They reached Rosie's street at the same time as Sid's patrol car drove toward them. He slowed, shooting them a glare.

"Oh, for goodness sake." Charlotte muttered. "When will he give up this nonsense?"

There was no answer as Rosie turned the corner. When Charlotte glanced down, the other woman's lips were tight together. Nothing changed until they reached Rosie's house.

"I love your garden." Charlotte smelled a flower. "What is this?"

"Freesia. Much of the garden is Graeme's work." Her smile was sad. "A legacy I love. Being a cottage style, many of the plants are perennial, so they die down over winter and bless me with beauty the next spring. Of course, autumn has its own share of flowers."

She opened the front door and wheeled inside, and Charlotte followed, closing and locking it.

"Do you always lock doors? We are in a country town." Rosie was already in the living room at the bar. "Same as last time?"

"Please. Remember I'm a city girl. My friend, Christie? She is married to a security fanatic—at least where she's concerned, but I think some of it rubbed off on me."

"I suppose with all the break-in's recently, there's merit in locking up when I'm home. I do though when I'm not here."

Mellow appeared through a cat door in a window, running to Rosie and jumping straight onto her lap.

"Hello my sweet. Where's your naughty brother?"

On cue, Mayhem slunk through the door, but did nothing more than acknowledge the humans were here with a twitch of his tail. Charlotte quite liked him. He had attitude.

"Here you go." Rosie held out a glass. "This one is made in the Barossa Valley. Although best knowns for its wines, there are a couple of lovely little gin distilleries as well. Graeme and I visited several times. Cheers."

"Cheers." Charlotte tapped glasses. "How long were you married, if that isn't too personal. I mean, tell me if I'm overstepping."

Rosie's smile was wide. "I love talking about Graeme. We married a little over forty years ago. Please, find a seat."

The moment Charlotte took a chair, Mellow joined her, curling up on her lap.

"Oh, she does like you! Graeme and I had a wonderful life together. We travelled a lot around Australia and overseas, often so we could indulge our love of deep-sea diving."

"Trev mentioned you used to do that. And that was where you lost your lower mobility."

"Stupid accident." Rosie almost gulped a mouthful, then sat for a moment, hand reached out to Mayhem, who surprisingly wandered across and allowed her to pet him. "Misjudged something and before I knew it, no feeling in my legs. Damned shame really."

"Very big damned shame."

"But we adjusted. Moved into this house and had it modified so I could function without too much outside assistance. Trev was young so it was hard on him, seeing his normally super-active mother relearning everything. Nobody thinks about things like the height a wheelchair has you, rather than your own legs."

Charlotte lifted her glass. "I am in awe. To you."

"Ha. I'll toast, but let's toast to us."

"Us?"

"Yup. Two strong women against the world."

"Two strong women, against the world."

They downed their glasses and laughed. It felt wonderful to let go of the stress and tension of the day. The cats purring became the only sound as Charlotte and Rosie fell into their own thoughts.

Rosie's head dropped as she stroked Mayhem's fur. He looked up at her and then stalked off with a growl. "Sorry, Mayhem." Rosie whispered.

"What's wrong?"

Tears poured down Rosie's face. She brushed them aside, but more came. Charlotte found a box of tissues and brought them to her, holding them out and sitting quietly to let Rosie cry. She swallowed to push down her responding empathy. Two people crying wasn't going to be a good look.

Mellow climbed onto Rosie's lap and tapped at the tears with her soft paw until Rosie had to laugh at her. With a handful of tissues, she dried the tears and blew her nose.

"Mayhem didn't like me spilling tears on him. But you," Rosie kissed Mellow's head, "you are a comfort."

"I'd wondered why he told you off."

Charlotte returned to her chair. Her heart went out to the other woman. Talking about her deceased husband and missing Trev had taken its toll.

"I feel a bit silly."

"Tears are good for you. They remove toxins amongst other things."

"Wish I could remove Octavia so easily." Rosie leaned back in her wheelchair. "What she said feels like a threat against the bookshop."

"Rosie, you own that building?"

"Yes. The whole of it, upstairs and downstairs."

"And the rates and stuff are all up to date?"

"Where are you going with this?" Rosie asked. "But yes, not a bill unpaid."

"I don't know her. Maybe she makes sweeping statements about people's livelihoods all the time, but if she can't touch the bookshop as an entity, then is she the type to try and stop customers shopping with you?"

Rosie held her hand out for Charlotte's empty glass and went to the bar. "She has some influence. The book club, for one. She is in quite a few organisations for that matter. Presumably, she can say negative things about the shop and turn people off."

"People who don't know you. Anyone who is a customer is hardly likely to change their buying habits based on the whispers of a grumpy woman."

"Small town rumours can be…lethal."

"Lethal?" Charlotte accepted the refilled glass. "Thanks. That's a considered word."

She was certain Rosie wanted to tell her something but wouldn't.

"Of course, I mean it could be the demise of a business. Look what some of them tried to do to the Christmas Tree farm. And I was speaking to a friend earlier who was up there to buy a tree and apparently they are getting almost no business."

"Perhaps it is just so close to Christmas?" Charlotte sipped her drink. She was enjoying these early evening chats here in this lovely home, even when they did become emotional.

"True. But Abbie made a comment about Darcy having to borrow some money to pay for the truck and helper to install the roundabout tree. Council aren't paying him until next year."

"That's outrageous!" Charlotte was certain her blood pressure just rose. "How can we help? I'm happy to buy groceries and take up, but will they accept them?"

Rosie shrugged. "You are so sweet, but I don't know how they'd respond. It would be nice to pull a whole package together for them, apart from the books already earmarked for Lachie."

The phone rang.

"Let it go to message." Rosie said. "I'll call them later."

For a while, they chatted about the shop and decided to again rearrange the front display window to entice more shoppers. Charlotte updated Rosie on the Facebook page, leaving out the negative review. No point upsetting her even more today.

"Why does Octavia think I'm Trev's girlfriend?" Charlotte had to ask. It had niggled at her all day. "Apart from the day he brought me to visit you, we've never been here together."

"Think about who else was in the shop that afternoon." Rosie said.

"Oh. Glenys. But she thought I worked there."

"And once she found out you didn't, she put her own slant on things."

"Well, I need to correct that." Charlotte's fingers tapped on her glass. "Which might also take the teeth out of Octavia's bite."

"Love that saying. But why bother? Your relationship with my son is nobody else's business, darling. Not even mine." Rosie grinned. "Although I'm all ears if you ever want to talk about him."

"Nope. Nothing to tell. Now, I might head home and see what I can make for dinner."

"You're most welcome to stay."

"Thank you. I have a bit to do though and need to practice cooking. You have no idea how ordinary I am when it comes to culinary arts." Charlotte took her glass into the kitchen and washed it. "So, don't ask me to cook anything for Christmas. I do salads though."

"Then, salads it is. Two if you have time." Rosie led the way to the front door and opened it. "I love having you here, Charlie. You're a good girl."

How could Charlotte tell her otherwise?

———

This time there were no strangers in masks outside the bookshop. No patrol car crawling past, or Sid smoking across the road. It was still light so maybe that was the key. Get home in light and stay inside.

How ridiculous.

Charlotte opened her laptop and searched a recipe site she'd found the other day. She might practise her salad skills for next week. Recipe selected, she dug around in the fridge. Everything was there except feta and Greek salad wasn't going to work without it.

At the bottom of the stairs she stopped. Almost dark, and by the time she returned, it would be. She glanced up the stairs, then shook her head and hurried to the street.

She rushed into the supermarket. Feta in hand, and a tub of yoghurt to go with some fresh fruit, she waited at the checkout. Two people ahead of her was a lady whose groceries had been packed into a bag, but her payment was rejected.

"I'm so sorry, I was sure this card had enough on it. I'll find some cash."

The cashier rolled her eyes.

Charlotte realised it was Abbie and bit her lip. Would she allow a virtual stranger to help? Abbie rummaged through her wallet, then her handbag, pulling out a couple of notes.

"This is really embarrassing. I thought I had a bit more cash. I'll need to take something out of the shopping. Um…"

"Excuse me." Charlotte reached her arm past the other customers. "I think you dropped this." She handed a twenty dollar note to the cashier in case Abbie refused it. "Nothing worse than dropping money in the supermarket."

Before anyone could do a thing, she stepped back and avoided eye contact. But someone was behind her in line now. She could smell him.

Sid Browne. Oh, joy.

A couple of minutes later she was through the checkout with her items. Abbie stood outside the supermarket, swapping her bags from one arm to another in discomfort. Charlotte grabbed them. "Where's your car?"

"You don't need—"

With a whisper, Charlotte nodded back to the supermarket. "Sid Browne's behind me and I'd appreciate being with you, if you don't mind."

Sid rounded the corner, looking each way. When he spotted Charlotte, he made a move her way.

"Car's over there, and thank you, this baby is kicking away at the moment and making everything twice as tricky!" Abbie grinned at Charlotte as though they were in a conspiracy, and together they crossed the road.

"Thank you, Abbie. He is the last person I want to engage with." Charlotte was conscious of him standing on the kerb watching them. "Is this one yours?"

"Until tomorrow. We've sold it and the new owner picks it up then."

The car was a late model hatch in great condition. There was a baby seat in the back. Abby popped the boot and Charlotte lifted the bags in. "You still have the flatbed?"

"Darcy needs that to deliver trees. But nowhere to put the baby seat and Lachie is only just big enough to ride in it with a booster seat. He's not the tallest of kids. You're Charlotte? You bought the little dried out tree."

"It is doing so well! The ends are green now and it gets some sunshine on the balcony."

"You really shouldn't have paid for it." Abbie rubbed her back with a small groan. "And about inside? As soon as we get paid for the car, I'll bring you the twenty dollars back. That was incredibly generous and discreet."

"Paying it forward. Big believer in it. Are you open on Sunday? I wouldn't mind taking a look at some more decorations and stuff."

"We are. Not that we've had many customers lately. It's almost as though people don't want to buy from us suddenly."

"I imagine people have their trees."

"Sure. Anyway, I need to get this home and feed my hungry boys." Abbie opened the driver's door. "Thank you. I mean it."

"Drive safely."

Charlotte waited until Abbie's car was out of sight before moving. She didn't want Sid following a pregnant woman at night.

Follow me, Senior Constable. I'll outrun you any day.

CHAPTER TWENTY-EIGHT

OH, HE'S REALLY GOING TO DO IT.

Charlotte strode along the footpath at a good pace without breaking into the run her brain was urging. She wasn't about to give Sid Browne a chance to speak to her, not when she was alone. Not to mention hungry.

He tried to keep pace from across the road. His puffing was audible and she considering asking if he needed an ambulance. Instead, she put her energy into keeping her face forward and getting her keys out of her pocket. If he followed her up the stairs, she had no intention of answering the door.

"Oi. Missy!"

Are you kidding me?

When she saw Trev next time, she'd ask what channel to pursue to make a formal complaint. Until that time, she was ignoring the man.

She passed the bookshop and turned into the driveway, now breaking into a jog to get up and inside as fast as possible. Heart pounding, she locked the door and rushed to the balcony, opening the sliding door just enough to slip through. She'd left the lights off and kept close to the wall as she edged to the railing.

Doubled over, Sid coughed as he heaved in oxygen on the opposite side of the road. A car pulled over but as the driver got out to check him, he suddenly straightened and waved the man away without so much as a thank you. Even from up here, it was obvious how unfit he was, and he'd not done as much as run. He coughed some more, hands on hips, then glared in the general direction of the balcony.

She kept still. His hand moved to his police belt and he glanced down to unclip a flashlight. Charlotte dived back into the apartment. No way was he catching her watching him. She turned on all the lights, including the balcony's lone light bulb. Then, she tapped her laptop to wake it up and selected some music. ABBA. Loud.

After pouring herself a glass of wine and sipping a few mouthfuls to settle her nerves, she got around to putting the yogurt into the fridge and getting the salad underway. Lots of olives. Half the block of feta, roughly chopped, and she did mean roughly. A tomato was stabbed into submission and the lettuce torn.

"Take that. And that."

If only Sid knew what she was doing, he'd probably arrest her for planning his demise. Death by ripping.

She sang along with some songs, letting the catchy music and words take the rest of the tension. If he was still out there, all he'd hear was her reasonably tuneful voice singing seventies songs and have nothing to see.

Once the salad looked pretty on the plate, she topped up her wine, turned off the music, and went onto the balcony. She turned off the overhead light and lit a candle on the table. Much nicer. The rows of coloured lights along the street slowly flashed from green to gold to red and back again. From somewhere down the road—maybe toward the restaurants—Christmas music carried.

She'd forgotten the dressing, so returned to the kitchen and mixed olive oil with balsamic vinegar in a bowl. Back at the table, she spooned some over the salad. Delicious. Yes, this was a definite for Christmas dinner.

Tomorrow she'd make a checklist of everything she had left to do before Christmas Day. Then, she had Sunday free to go shopping, and visit the Christmas Tree farm. Perhaps that was her opportunity to ensure the little family had enough. Because from the lack of money Abbie had at the supermarket and selling their only child-friendly car, the signs pointed to a difficult festive season.

———

The first hour the bookshop was open saw no customers. Not one. Rosie and Charlotte had both brought lunch with them and expected to be run off their feet until the earlier Saturday closing time of four.

"Is this her doing?" Rosie muttered under her breath as she peered out the window for the third time.

"Rosie, come and have your coffee because once the rush begins, you'll have no chance. And no, Octavia Morris does not control the buying habits of a whole community, especially not after one day."

"How did you hear me?"

"I have super-hearing. Just one of my superpowers."

Unable to do anything but smile, Rosie wheeled around the counter to her usual spot. "What are the other ones? These superpowers?"

"You'll find out over time. They mostly revolve around being bossy in times of crisis. Ask your son."

Rosie shot her a look with her eyebrows raised, but Charlotte did a zipping motion across her mouth. "That's all I'm saying."

"You are being quite mean. Using my son to get my attention then refusing to divulge why. I will ask him." She picked up her coffee and drank.

"See. Isn't that better? Now, you enjoy that, and I'll fill you in on the events of last night after I left you."

In a few sentences, Charlotte told Rosie about her chance meeting with Abbie and her thoughts about the financial situation up at the farm. She left out mention of Sid.

"Well, I'm sorry to hear Abbie had trouble at the register, but thankful you were there. I admit to worrying about that little family. They might have been better to sell the place when Darcy's dad passed on, rather than try and regenerate a sinking business."

"Why would they leave their own home and come here? It seems risky." Charlotte picked up her own coffee."

"Family pride. Darcy has volumes of belief in hard work, responsibility, and doing the right thing. He'd have been heartbroken at the state the place got into and if there are outstanding rates to pay, he'd want to pay them."

"Is there a market up here for properties so large?"

Rosie nodded. "Always. We're one of those fast growth regions and council don't seem to mind encouraging it. So far though the town has overturned a few of their planning decisions, but a big parcel of land like Darcy's would surely attract developers."

"Not a fan of some developers."

"Do you mean the one your friend was engaged to? Christie? Didn't he try to sink the yacht she was on or something?"

"Yes. Quite an interesting personality mix in him. Narcissist with sociopath tendencies. And really cunning." Charlotte stared into the distance. "The sort of patient I'd love to have but would end up walking away from."

"What do you think of me?"

Charlotte turned to Rosie with a frown. "I don't actually analyse everyone I meet. And never you, or anyone I care about. Not unless they have asked for help and I need more insight."

"But I'm curious."

"From the look of things, we're about to have company." Thank goodness. "But I will say the two words that make me smile about you."

"Oh? Crazy cat lady? That's three. Or, world's best boss?"

"Which is also three. I had no idea your maths was so bad."

People stepped out of a car parked outside.

"I was thinking along the lines of tough cookie." Charlotte said.

Rosie thought about it. "I do like cookies."

"Careful or I shall analyse you. Come on, time to make a whole lot of money." Charlotte grinned and got up to greet the customers as they wandered in. "Good morning! How may I help this lovely day?"

CHAPTER TWENTY-NINE

At the busiest part of the day, a tall man and very short lady waited patiently at the counter as both Rosie and Charlotte contended with what felt like an endless stream of customers. Rosie took money and chatted. Charlotte gift wrapped.

Rosie had acknowledged the couple and asked if they minded waiting, so there they stayed, for at least ten minutes. When at last there was a break at the counter, although Charlotte continued roaming the shop from customer to customer, Rosie had reached her hand out to shake theirs.

"Charlie, this is Pastor and Mrs Stevens. They are generously helping with the giving box. Pastor, Mrs Stevens, please meet Charlotte Dean who recently joined me here."

That done, Charlotte took off to take books from someone with a tower in their arms and missed much of the conversation. The next time she looked, they'd left, and the giving box was empty. Not for long though, with two more donations—this time with a request the books go to a residential aged home—straight back in the box.

The shop empty again, Charlotte flopped onto her stool and gulped some water.

"You are a little powerhouse, darling. Two more hours then a whole day to recover!"

"Gonna need it! So, your visitors took everything?"

"They run a local charity and although I'm not personally a church goer, have seen the wonderful work they've done in the community in the past. I've every confidence they'll spread the love around."

"But we've still got the books for Lachie?"

"Of course. And look at the collection!"

Charlotte turned around. On the back counter were seven, no eight gift wrapped books for him. They ranged from the latest age-appropriate fiction to a biography of a sportsperson he apparently liked, and a very cool book about young entrepreneurs. That should keep him busy for a while.

"What about his parents?" she asked.

"I don't know Abbie very well so don't know what she likes. And Darcy is not a reader."

"What if we put together a hamper? Things for the new baby, plus some Christmas goodies they might not splash out on." Charlotte suggested. "I'm going up there tomorrow, so maybe I can get some ideas."

"Are you being a sleuth again?"

"Probably. The problem is timing. If I discover items they might use that aren't available in Kingfisher Falls, there's little time left to shop elsewhere."

"Or, a gift voucher. The supermarkets all sell them."

"What a good idea!"

Marguerite Browne walked past the shop. Halfway past the second window she turned and made her way inside. Charlotte and Rosie exchanged a glance.

"Right." Marguerite said as she leaned on the counter with both hands. "You're both here. Excellent."

"How may we help, Mrs Browne?" Charlotte stood, a smile on her face.

"I don't need your help."

"If you are going to be rude, Marguerite —" Rosie started.

"No! No, please don't think that for one minute! I really don't need Carol's help."

"Charlotte."

"Anyway, I came to apologise on behalf of the Kingfisher Falls Bookclub. And Octavia, although she won't admit it."

Rosie laced her fingers together. "Really."

"I wasn't here to know exactly what was said, but from Octavia's account, there was a misunderstanding about the ordering of the books for our next meeting."

"Not a misunderstanding, but please continue."

"She was worried we wouldn't have time to receive the books in question, get them to our members, and organise one of our nights. December is such a busy month and then in January, a lot of the ladies go away on holiday, so the dates are quite critical."

"I appreciate that, Marguerite. Really, I do understand the timing, but it is out of my control. I'd love to provide the books for you as I have done for so many years." Rosie was calm and still. "Whatever happens, my commitment to the readers of Kingfisher Falls hasn't wavered, and you really should know that."

Marguerite wouldn't meet Rosie's eyes. "Um. Of course. You are a valued member of the community."

"But Octavia said otherwise. She really hurt my feelings, in fact. And for the record, I have nothing at all against you. Or Sid. I only judge people by the things they do, not who they really are."

That's my Rosie.

"She shouldn't have raised the past." Marguerite straightened. "What happened back then is best forgotten. Don't you agree? Anyway, it is almost Christmas. A time for family. Well, except for poor Octavia who really does feel alone at this time of year since Darcy's mother stole her husband away."

"No doubt Darcy's father felt the same about Octavia's husband, but as you say, it is almost Christmas and I believe it is a perfect opportunity to show our generosity. Pastor and Mrs Stevens have collected most of the contents of the giving box, and I'd love to refill it by Christmas Eve." Rosie gestured to the box with a smile. "Do you know we also donate five dollars from every book put into the box?"

Marguerite narrowed her eyes. "Nice of you. And where will those funds go?"

"We haven't decided, but there is a small family who are doing it tough this year and could benefit from some community support." Rosie said.

"I will buy another book, but neither it nor the donation are to go to the Forests. If that's who you refer to." Marguerite flicked through some discounted books near the counter.

Charlotte opened her mouth to respond, but Rosie beat her to it.

"As I won't guarantee that, nor be dictated to in my own shop, I'd suggest you don't partake in this charitable venture unless you have a heart open to the plight of those less fortunate than themselves. Whoever they are."

How Rosie said it with such sweetness and calmness was beyond Charlotte, who was about to say something similar, but in very plain terms.

Hand on a book, Marguerite froze. A flush of red rose from her neck to her face and she snatched her hand away as though bitten. Without another word or look, she stalked out of the shop.

"Whoops." Rosie didn't sound the least bit concerned.

"You are officially my hero." Charlotte said. "Who does that? Offers charity as long as it excludes the very people who need it."

Rosie gazed out to the street. Marguerite was out of sight. "I fear I've made things worse. Whatever little step we took forward, we just fell backwards over the cliff."

"You stood up for the shop. And your ethics. You can only control your own actions, not theirs."

Pay attention, Charlie. Applies to you also.

CHAPTER THIRTY

RETALIATION CAME QUICKLY. WITHIN A FEW MINUTES, SID SET UP a breathalyser stop outside the bookshop. He parked his patrol car out from the kerb, its lights flashing, then cordoned off several parking spaces with witches' hats. But then he did nothing other than lean back on the bonnet of his car and stare into the shop.

The rush of customers slowed to a trickle. People complained of needing to park much further away and walk back. Rosie and Charlotte apologised to customers for the inconvenience more than sold books, or so it seemed.

"Shouldn't have said anything." Rosie glared at Sid and he waved.

"Ignore him. That's all I do."

"Meaning?" Rosie wheeled to the back of the shop with a lap full of books. "What's he done now?"

"Oh, I just mean when I come across him like this. He wants you to bite."

"This is one of my busiest days of the year and he does this." She began stocking a low shelf, her hands shaking.

Charlotte took the books from her. "We need to do something

about him. If I leave the shop, he'll probably follow me. Should I try it?"

Rosie sighed. "No. You are right, and I should focus on getting everything as nice as possible in here while it isn't too busy. Monday will be like nothing you've seen...unless he does that again."

"You know what? If he does, I'll go for a walk somewhere. Even if it means you coping alone for a little bit."

"But what if he stops you?"

With a laugh, Charlotte got to her feet. "I might have once told Trev I'm not a runner, but I can certainly out move a certain unfit police officer."

"Unfit in more than one way."

"We should make an anonymous call that there's a carton of cigarettes waiting on his doorstep."

"I'm shocked, Charlie!" Rosie couldn't keep a straight face. "Only a carton?"

Both women burst into laughter.

Sid crossed his arms and stepped closer.

"Does he think we're laughing at him?" Charlotte almost choked as she struggled to control her giggles.

"I hope so."

He was now at the window, peering in.

"We're going to be arrested for laughing without a permit." Rosie waved to him. "Or whatever nonsense he comes up with."

For an instant it did look as though Sid would storm in. Instead, he turned around and packed up the witches' hats, throwing them into the boot and slamming it down. A moment later he drove off, almost hitting another car coming from behind him.

"Oh my." Rosie's hand went to her mouth.

"Yes. And this is local law enforcement."

"Thank goodness he's moved on."

Charlotte agreed, but her gut told her this was far from the end of the interference from Sid and the book club ladies.

———

There was a sudden thunderstorm not long after Rosie left for the day. Charlotte hoped she'd made it home before the rain came. The day's takings were disappointing, only boosted by the busy couple of hours in the morning and a last-minute customer who purchased two series and then donated three autobiographies to the giving box.

As much as Rosie had brushed off Sid's attempt to hurt the business today, and Marguerite's odd visit, Charlotte had seen the distress in her eyes, the forced smiles as the day went on.

This kind and gentle woman didn't deserve such appalling treatment. That Sid was a police officer made it more offensive to Charlotte. He was supposed to protect people from the bad guys, not be one himself.

Laptop open to distract herself from the storm, Charlotte visited the bookshop's Facebook page. A few new page likes. But there were more reviews. Bad ones.

Tried to make me donate to their cause. Refused to serve me when I wouldn't.

Asked for books to be ordered and was told to go elsewhere.

Not friendly.

Owner laughed at person with a disability.

"What the hell?" Charlotte couldn't believe what she was reading. Unless it was Sid and he thought he had one, but who on earth would say this of a wheelchair-bound woman? The first three statements were from *Annoyed Customer, Shocked Customer, Sad Customer.*

"Make that Marguerite Browne, Octavia Morris, and possibly Glenys Lane." Charlotte murmured.

The fourth name was *Disenworb the Greatest.* "Not just great?"

She flicked to first bad review from the other day—*Disenworb the Great.*

None of the names were clickable, so either they'd set their privacy setting to stop her seeing their pages or were fake accounts. Or both.

Something made her take screenshots of the comments. She saved these in a file she named *Christmas Tree Thief.* Next, Charlotte searched Facebook for the names attributed to the reviews. The two *Disenworb* pages existed. Both set up in the last week and neither with any other information. She reported the pages to Facebook as fake accounts.

Thunder rattled the windows and Charlotte glanced out of the window. It was almost dark from the cloud cover as rain bucketed down. She shivered even though it was warm enough and focused on the laptop, typing in Sid's name.

His face came up as the profile image. Charlotte scrolled through some of his posts, wishing she hadn't when she came across racist memes and support for certain political parties with dreadful human rights policies. Tired of it, she clicked on his friends list. There weren't many. No names she recognised from her limited knowledge of the locals. All this told her was stuff she could guess.

There was a bio. *Sid Browne—the Greatest.*

She grabbed a pen and wrote out *Disenworb*. "Hah! Sid and Browne spelt backwards." Charlotte took a screenshot of the top of his page, then reported it. Might as well put him under some scrutiny. She saved that screenshot in her new file.

This was getting somewhere, although she had no idea quite where. Presumably the police department had rules about social media and their staff. It felt important she kept records of anything she discovered about Sid.

Before closing Facebook, Charlotte searched for the book club ladies. None of them kept accounts from what she could find.

Finally, the Christmas Tree farm. To her surprise there was a business page for it, although an old one. There were no new posts for some months and those were from Darcy introducing himself and asking customers to watch out for updates on opening times.

The cover photo was beautiful. Taken at sunrise, light filtered through the pine trees to the house. It was inviting and showed a home once well maintained and loved. How sad it had fallen into disrepair. The star rating of the business was two out of five. More of the nasty lies from the bookshop page and over a period of weeks. If this was the work of Sid Browne, one had to ask why. And if he hated the Forests so much, was he behind the thefts? And if so, exactly how was Charlotte going to prove it?

CHAPTER THIRTY-ONE

OVERNIGHT THE STORM PASSED, LEAVING A CLEAR SKY AND THE coolest air since Charlotte arrived in Kingfisher Falls. She stood at the pool beneath the falls as the sun rose, casting the first rays through the forest around her.

The falls almost thundered, swollen from the rain and filling the pool until it was level with the ground around it. Water flowed faster in the narrow river, which was also much higher than her last visit.

She breathed deeply, inhaling a mixture of scents, from eucalypts and ferns to the water itself. A small mob of kangaroos hopped to the edge of the pond, not the least worried by Charlotte's presence. She stayed still, not wishing to startle them, nor be turned on if they saw her as a threat.

One by one they drank. She counted nine, including a joey which popped its head out of a pouch to blink at Charlotte through curious eyes. If only she'd brought her phone, she could take pictures. But that's what the brain was for. Keeping precious memories like this.

Unless you have Mother's diseases.

As the kangaroos moved off, she wished she was free like them. No fears of being a genetic walking timebomb. Nothing to stop her living life to the fullest. Falling in love. Having her own family. Remembering them when she was old.

Grief kicked her in the guts. She put both hands on her stomach and pressed lightly, eyes closed. Until she found the courage to take the genetic tests to find out, her life was on hold. Any thoughts of a family to love were unwelcome reminders of what she probably would never have. It wouldn't be fair to them.

"It wasn't fair to me." Saying it helped. That's what she always told her patients. Say the fears aloud to take away their power. "I'm scared." This was a whisper. "I don't know what to do."

From the pond came a different sound. A high-pitched whistle of *pee-ee, pee-ee,* a thin but piercing sound broke her thoughts apart and she opened her eyes.

On a branch above the pond, and only a few metres away, a small bird watched her. A second later it dived and, in a motion, almost too fast for Charlotte's eyes, captured a tiny fish. It flew past, its wings a vivid blue, with yellow on its neck and a long black bill.

Only when it disappeared did she work out what she'd just seen. An Azure Kingfisher.

———

Charlotte's car bumped along the road to the Christmas Tree farm without incident. No sign of speeding utes or law enforcement—if you could still call Sid that. There were no cars going either way. Only Charlotte. She glanced at the clock on the dashboard. Was ten too early?

After seeing the kingfisher, she'd floated home. What an incredible moment. The little endangered bird with its bold whistle and speed was unbelievably beautiful. Charlotte knew it wasn't endangered worldwide, but here, from what she'd been told and read, it was rare to see them.

She parked in an otherwise empty carpark. This time, she concentrated on her environment. On two sides of the carpark, the trees were tall, creating a natural and peaceful boundary. They were cleared on the third side to make way for the sheds and sales area.

And then there was the house. Still striking with its two floors overlooking the valley on the other side, its paint was peeling and the garden around it overgrown.

"Pretty rundown, huh?" Darcy appeared from the trees behind her with a grimace. "I'll fix it. Just got other things to fix first."

"Hi Darcy. I was admiring your house. What an amazing view you must have."

"If there was ever time to enjoy it." He carried a chainsaw. "Sorry. Been one of those weeks and now I find this out in the middle of the trees."

"The chainsaw?"

Darcy headed for the sheds and Charlotte caught up.

"Why was it out there?"

"Asking myself the same thing. This was stolen a couple of weeks ago from the back of my truck. Had to buy another. At this time of year." His voice gave away a frustration and anger. "What kind of person steals a man's livelihood?"

Let me guess...

"We're doing our best up here and don't hurt a soul, no matter what some of the gossips say."

"Ignore them is my advice. The bookshop's Facebook page is being trolled by fake accounts with a bunch of lies right now."

Darcy gave her a look of disbelief. "The bookshop? Even worse. Rosie is one of a kind and always there for anyone who needs a hand. Has this whole town lost the plot?"

"Where was the truck when this was stolen?"

"Um...far end of the northern boundary, I think. Yeah. I'd been cutting back some undergrowth near Glenys's fence line. This time of year, fire is a risk and with all the other stuff I've had to do, controlling the undergrowth was miles behind."

They passed the sales shed. There was no sign of any movement there. Then, toward a large shed further back.

"So, you were using the chainsaw and then it disappeared?"

"Are you a police officer?" Darcy grinned.

"Sorry, don't mean to interrogate. No, just someone who is a bit alarmed by what's going on around this town."

"Okay. I tossed it on the back and went to where I'd been cutting. It took maybe half an hour for me to drag a heap of branches back with me to bring back to my mulcher. Didn't even notice it missing until I got back. Damned annoying."

They were at the shed and Darcy went straight in. "I'll be right back." He took the chainsaw to a long workbench and left it there. The shed was huge, holding a tractor, his flatbed truck, and an assortment of tools. Charlotte stepped back so it didn't look like she was casing it.

On his way out, he pulled the door closed and locked it. "Can't lose anything else."

"Darcy, last question. The chainsaw—you said you found it just now. Was it anywhere near where it disappeared?"

"Other side of the property and under some old branches. It didn't get there on its own."

"No idea who took it?"

He shook his head. "Thought it had fallen of the back and I spent hours looking for it. Gave up and got another one. Who would take it and then leave it where I'd find it?"

Who indeed.

"I know you must think I'm nosy, but I have seen the work of these Christmas Tree thieves close up. They had a chainsaw, Darcy. I wonder if it is worth having yours fingerprinted?"

Darcy folded his arms, deep in thought. All was quiet apart from birdsong in the trees. "Short of taking it out of the area to find someone who could help, what good will it do? Sid Morris won't do anything."

"Why though? Does anyone ever ask him why he won't pursue a lead?"

"Not if you want to stay off his radar. Now, I've taken up a lot of your time, but I haven't asked how I can help you? How's the poor little tree you bought?"

Charlotte smiled. "I think it might be growing. Bit by bit, it is looking healthier. Gets a bit of sun and plenty of encouragement. I thought I'd see what else you have in the way of gifts as I'm short on what I've got so far."

"Come and see. I've done a bit of woodwork now it's so quiet." He led the way to the sales shed.

"Will you make things to order?"

"Sure. What do you have in mind?"

"Wind chimes. Lovely big ones."

"Never tried those. Let me have a play and see if my equipment lets me do the tubes."

Lachie was behind the long table, straightening rows of tinsel.

"Hey mate, where's Mum?"

"Mrs Forest was on the phone, so I came ahead." Lachie gazed at Charlotte. "I remember you."

"I remember you also. Lachie Forest, chief helper."

A broad smile filled his face.

"Darcy?" Abbie's voice drifted from near the house.

"Up here, babe." Darcy called. "Back in a minute."

Once Darcy was out of sight, Lachie's smile faded. "Mum's upset. The man with car isn't coming now."

"Oh. The man who was buying it?"

"Uh huh. She didn't know I was there, but she told him if he didn't buy it, we might lose our home. And there'd be nothing for Christmas." He rolled some baubles as he spoke, eyes following them as they tapped each other along the table.

Charlotte's chest ached for the little boy.

Lachie didn't know there was a pile of brand-new books coming his way. At least he'd have those to open. And Charlotte was certain Rosie intended to use the donation money to help the Forest family.

"Something good will happen, Lachie. I promise you —"

"I'd rather you don't, Charlotte." Darcy strode toward the shed. His face was blank. "Don't promise what can't be." He went to the cash register and opened the drawer. "Abbie mentioned you helped her out at the supermarket, and I thank you for doing such a kind deed."

He held out a twenty-dollar bill for Charlotte.

"Not necessary. And hope is important, particularly..." she glanced at Lachie, who still played with the baubles.

"Reality is important." Darcy's voiced was strained, and his eyes showed a defeat that hurt Charlotte to see. "Please."

She took the note.

"We have each other and that's what matters, hey mate?" Darcy put his hand on Lachie's shoulder as if his son was a lifeline. "We don't need charity."

"It wasn't…but I—"

"Come on, Lachie, let's go give your mother a hand."

The message was loud and clear. Charlotte nodded and walked across the carpark to her car. Pride was all Darcy had at this moment. She slid behind the wheel. Abbie was at the edge of the carpark near the house and when Lachie and Darcy reached her, they wrapped their arms around each. Abbie's shoulders shuddered as she sobbed.

But Darcy had more than pride. He had a family.

Charlotte drove out of the carpark slowly, unable to stem the tide of tears that came from a deep and lonely part of her heart.

CHAPTER THIRTY-TWO

BACK HOME, CHARLOTTE HAD A LONG SHOWER. HER MISSION TO get ideas for ways to help the Forests had failed. They needed more than she or the town could give them, and besides, would they even accept a helping hand?

As water poured over her head, she closed her eyes, digging deep inside for the pain awakened so unexpectedly by Lachie, then reinforced by seeing the family supporting each other. Her heart hurt for them and every bit as much for herself but it was okay. Now she'd found it, she could deal with it. She'd never experienced the kind of family love the Forests shared.

But it wasn't your fault. You were a little girl filled with love. And you are worth loving.

She repeated it in her mind a few times, then aloud, letting the emotions wash away with the shower water. When she turned off the tap, a sense of calmness settled on her. This was progress.

Wrapped in a towel, Charlotte went into the spare bedroom and touched the box on the bed. It wasn't time to open this yet. But she knew she was one step closer to exploring the past her mother had hidden away from her for so long. In the week off work following Christmas, she'd start sorting through the secrets. For whatever reasons, Angelica Dean had hung onto bits of her own past, and that of her daughter's. Maybe those reasons would become clear once Charlotte let herself look.

For now, though, there was a lot to do in a very small space of time. Closing the door on the bedroom with the box, Charlotte went to her own room and dressed in pants and shirt. If she was to complete her gift shopping, she needed to get on with it. She made a list of people to buy for and what to get.

Rosie (cat gifts/teapot)

Trev (no idea whatsoever)

Esther and Doug (almost no idea. Maybe a bottle of wine? Or movie tickets?)

The Forest Family

Charlotte was stuck on the last one even more than the others. What she really wanted was to give them all the trappings of a Christmas dinner plus presents. But she barely knew them and understood she was partly responding to her own feelings about their situation.

As she drove out of Kingfisher Falls a little later, she argued with herself.

Darcy was adamant he wanted no charity.

But a Christmas gift was not charity.

If she rocked up with a hamper of goodies, the family might be embarrassed because they had nothing to give in return or thought they were viewed as a cause.

On the other hand, hampers were popular gift choices for people who had everything.

She liked that.

The road she followed was new to her, heading across to the town of Gisborne. Once she'd found cat toys, then she'd return to Kingfisher Falls to buy the rest in her own town. She also had a shopping list so on Christmas Day she could make perfect salads and take them to Rosie's in the evening.

As she stopped at a T-junction to turn, a car pulled up behind her. A dark blue car. She told herself not to jump at shadows because through the mirrors it could as easily be a sedan as a ute. But the tint was too dark to see inside. And she knew it was illegal to tint the windscreen like that.

She turned when traffic allowed and watched her mirrors. When the car behind followed, her heart jumped. It was a ute. The ute.

————

Stay calm. Drive normally.

There were no plates on the ute. It trailed her but not so close as to be dangerous so it might be a coincidence it was travelling the same way.

By the time she reached the 'Gisborne' sign, she'd decided it was that. Two vehicles using the same road. Even though one had no plates, illegal tinting, and probably was the ute involved in the thefts. If they went their own way soon, she'd be okay.

She found her destination and parked not far from the shop. The ute drove past with no sign of slowing. For a few minutes she stayed in the car. It didn't return. The road was quite visible in both directions, with a carpark across the road, so she was sure she'd see the ute if it was around.

Time was getting away, so she took a deep breath and got out, locking the car before going shopping. She adored the shop, with its friendly staff and selection of products, but spent less time there than she'd otherwise do. At least now she had some goodies for Mayhem and Mellow.

Back in the car, she drove around the block to take a quick look at the town. Around the same size as Kingfisher Falls, this was another pretty village. The ute was parked outside a supermarket. Something made her pull into an empty parking space. She grabbed her phone and the door handle, ready to get some photos of the ute and hoping nobody was inside.

But two men emerged from the supermarket carrying cartons of beer. She opened the camera app and started taking photos. Their heights and builds reminded her of the men in the masks. They put the cartons into the back of the ute, talking to each other. They were young. Early twenties at the most. They got in and a moment later, backed the ute out.

Charlotte threw her phone back into her handbag and eased out of her parking spot after letting another car pass. The ute sped away and she followed around the next corner.

It was disappearing fast along the road and she wasn't about to lose it. Or speed.

Patience.

A car pulled out in front and slowed her down.

"Not now."

Her fingers tapped on the steering wheel until she found a safe place to pass. The speed limit increased as the road left town and Charlotte touched the accelerator.

Where are you?

At the end of a long curve she finally saw the ute. She doubted if she could match its pace, but if she didn't completely lose sight, she might find out where they lived. Adrenalin coursed through her and she told herself to stay focused. This was the break she'd needed.

Where would they lead her to?

Glenys's property? Maybe they were her relatives doing dirty work on her behalf. Glenys had been so cutting about the Forest family in the bookshop that time. And she lived next door to the farm so who knew if there were neighbourly issues. There was something secretive about Glenys Lane.

Or were they associated with Sid after all? He'd certainly ignored the ute even after Charlotte pointed out it had just damaged her windscreen, and he had no interest in investigating any evidence from the roundabout or Esther's shop.

"I bet these two belong to you, Octavia Morris!"

Who else had such a grudge against the Christmas Tree Farm? She lived and breathed her hatred of the family, even though her own husband was as much to blame for the breakdown of the marriages. These young men might be her grandsons or hired help. And now they were on their way to her house to celebrate all the chaos they'd created.

Charlotte was puzzled when the ute turned off before Kingfisher

Falls. She was sure Octavia lived on the other side of town. Keeping her distance, she followed. The street was familiar but the last thing she'd expected was the ute to turn into the carpark in front of the garden supplies building.

Stealing more trees, gentlemen?

She nosed her car alongside the kerb on the street, far enough away to hopefully avoid being spotted watching them, and got her camera set up.

The passenger got out, spoke to the driver, then closed the door.

Now the ute was moving again. Charlotte took a couple of quick photos and was about to start the motor to follow when Veronica emerged from the shop. Charlotte almost dropped the phone as the young man pulled Veronica against himself and kissed her on the lips. Her arms went around his waist and she kissed him back.

Oh. My. Goodness.

Even as her mind formed the words, she was snapping images. She needed evidence, some means of connecting the ute, the men, and Veronica. And although she had no idea how to report this, or what step was next, Charlotte knew in her gut she'd found the Christmas Tree thief.

CHAPTER THIRTY-THREE

CHARLOTTE STAYED IN HER CAR FOR A LONG TIME. A QUICK glance at the clock on the dashboard told her it was only ten minutes, but each one of those minutes dragged. Watching Veronica and the young man make out turned her stomach, for no other reason than knowing these were the people behind a whole lot of hurt in and out of town.

After a while, the kissing stopped and talking began. There was laughing and gesturing as the man described something in detail. Charlotte took the odd photo but didn't know what she was going to do with them. She wasn't a detective and might be considered a stalker or pervert now.

She imagined showing these to Sid. Would he fall over from laughing, or slap her into handcuffs? If Trev was here, he'd take her seriously. After he'd told her off for putting herself in danger following a suspicious vehicle. And keeping secrets.

Yet that's what she did best. Keep secrets. Err on the side of caution every time. At least now she did, after the mess she'd made of her life and her patient's life in Queensland.

The phone went back in her handbag. There was nothing she could do. What proof was there that Veronica was involved in this anyway, other than by having some romantic relationship with one of the thieves.

You can't even prove he's one of them.

Her heart sank. All this excitement for nothing. It would take a lot more than a few photos and a statement to catch a criminal.

A car and trailer pulled into the carpark and after a family climbed out and went into the shop, Veronica kissed the man again and then followed them inside. He made a phone call and began walking back toward town.

Very carefully, Charlotte trailed him. She waited until he was almost out of sight, then drove at a crawl, hugging the kerb, until she had a clear view. This she repeated until the blue ute appeared from the other direction, did a U-turn, and picked him up. By the time she accelerated and got to where he'd been, the ute was gone.

————

Frustration sent Charlotte home after half an hour of fruitless searching the neighbourhood for a sign of the ute. She carried her purchases from Gisborne upstairs and left them on the sofa. She still had much shopping to do and worrying about Veronica and her friend was getting her riled up with no means of resolving it.

Bags in hand, she ran downstairs ready to enjoy the rest of the afternoon. She promised herself a picnic at the waterfall if she stayed on track now. Perhaps the kingfisher would show itself again.

The bookshop might be closed, but most of the other shops in town were open to capture the last of the Christmas shopping frenzy. Esther was busy with customers as Charlotte passed her shop but managed a quick smile and wave. A few doors along was a lovely little liquor store and to Charlotte's relief, the assistance knew exactly what Esther and Doug liked to drink.

One down.

Was Trev really coming up here for Christmas?

Charlotte stopped outside the liquor store. If so, she really needed to have a gift for him, but what? Nothing that said, 'I missed you', or 'there's a future'. Nope. No false hopes being handed out.

More along the lines of, 'nice to see you, person-who-is-a-bit-more-than-an-acquaintance'.

How about, 'Merry Christmas. I enjoy your company'.

Slightly better.

She headed for the homeware shop with no idea what she was searching for.

"Hello! You must be Rosie's new assistant."

The voice came from the back of the shop, but it wasn't until Charlotte looked up that she found the source. At the top of a ladder against the back wall, a man grinned down at her. In his late sixties, he had a full head of white hair and white eyebrows above small spectacles.

Charlotte couldn't help smiling in return as she made her way to the bottom of the ladder. He climbed down with surprising sprightliness and shot out his hand for her to shake.

"Greetings and welcome to Kingfisher Falls," his voice had a distinctive English accent. "I'm Lewis, owner of this little shop of offerings"

"Nice to meet you, Lewis. And yes, I'm Charlotte and work for Rosie."

"The way I hear it, you are working *with* her, not for." His smile was genuine and his eyes sparkled over the spectacles.

How had she not met this lovely man yet? Charlotte gazed around. "This is such a nice shop! I've looked through the windows at night a few times but had no idea you have so much in here."

"Then please spend as much time browsing as you wish. Do you have something in mind?"

"I do love the ceramic teapots."

"For you, or a gift?"

"I thought for Rosie."

"Indeed! Shall we take a closer look?" Without waiting for an answer, Lewis was off.

At the counter half an hour later, Charlotte's mind was a whirlwind of patterns, colours, brands, and materials. Not just for the gorgeous teapot set Lewis was now gift wrapping, but for a couple of gifts she'd bought for herself. And one for Trev, which she still wasn't sure about. It wasn't for wrapping yet. Not until she'd decided.

"So, you mentioned earlier you've been window shopping at night?" Lewis unravelled a long piece of red ribbon with snowflakes and snipped the end.

"Yes, after work. I'm trying to find my way around. There are a few empty shops. Is that normal?"

He frowned. "No. But this past year there's been people opening, shutting, opening, shutting all over the place."

"What kind of shops?"

Lewis released the ribbon and it curled back on itself. "Excellent question, Charlotte. Have you seen the shoe shop?"

"Around the corner?"

"Yes. Another shoe shop opened next door to it."

"Wow, that's a bit close."

He leaned toward Charlotte with none of the earlier sparkle in his eyes. "They are a good business and the intruder closed in weeks. We had a drink and sighed in relief for our fellow long-time trader. A week later, the same person moved in next door."

"Next door, here? With the shoes again?"

"No, my dear. With giftware. Kitchenware. All kinds of things for the home." Lewis gestured around his shop with both arms. "Not good products as mine are. Cheap stuff."

Charlotte's mind raced back to the garden centre. Those boxes piled along the far wall. What was scribbled on them? Shoes. Clothes. Saucepans. Books.

"Veronica."

"How do you know this?" Lewis raised both eyebrows. "I didn't mention her."

Charlotte filled him in on what she'd seen. "Did she explain herself? Targeting shops by moving in next door with the same products?"

Lewis sniffed. "Not the same. Cheap. But that…lady, gave no explanation. She even had the nerve to start rumours that I was closing down. As if that would happen!" He picked up the ribbon and began tying it around the present.

"I don't know a lot about retail but would imagine there is a fair amount of cost setting up a shop. And then paying rent?" Charlotte bit her bottom lip. Was this the motive for the break-ins, some kind of revenge for the town not supporting her?

"She would have had some costs, mainly the stock, but she didn't bother with nice stands, or anything to enhance the customer experience. And rent? Both landlords offered her a rent-free period."

"And she closed before that ended. So, there are landlords out of pocket as well." Charlotte said. "Did she already have the garden centre?"

"There you are, all beautifully wrapped for dear Rosie." He gently placed the box closer to Charlotte. "As for Veronica? She had already chased off most of the garden centre's customers with her lack of attentiveness and if I may say, rudeness."

Oh, you may!

"I have enjoyed meeting you, Lewis." Charlotte offered her hand over the counter.

"And I, you. Shall I expect to see you at the Christmas Eve party?"

"Um, I didn't know about it."

"Ah. After we close tomorrow night, many of us gather in the plaza for a get-together. Very informal. Both restaurants are closed because they do Christmas lunches, so we all bring a plate of something nice and share it around. Our little tradition."

"Sounds lovely. Merry Christmas."

Back outside, Charlotte decided to leave grocery shopping for first thing in the morning, before work. She had her hands full with bags and boxes, so made her way home. It was time to look at the photos she'd taken.

CHAPTER THIRTY-FOUR

CHARLOTTE CLOSED HER LAPTOP. SHE'D UPLOADED HER PHOTOS to see them on the larger screen and search for any clues to help. But there was nothing. Lots of images of Veronica at different angles, quite a few of her boyfriend. The ute. No luck at all with the driver.

She'd gone further back to the night of Esther's window being broken but shards of glass told her nothing. Even the images from the roundabout were of little value. There were several photos of the men as they pulled down the tree, but none were face on and it was difficult to tell if one was indeed the passenger from earlier.

Nothing to prove the man with Veronica was even there.

If only Charlotte had seen their faces when the masks came off at the bookshop. Or if one of them had turned around at the roundabout.

She had no ideas about what to do next and nobody to bounce ideas off.

Before her head exploded, she needed to fulfil that promise to herself and visit the waterfall.

She changed into shorts and T-shirt, grabbed a hat, and threw a sandwich and water bottle into a backpack. In minutes she was striding out in the warm air, longing to get to the steps and work off the tension of the morning. Although she'd planned to have an evening picnic, she'd missed lunch, so mid-afternoon sandwich at the falls it was.

The further she walked, the clearer her thoughts became. Finding the bad guys wasn't her job. It was Sid's. If he failed to fulfil his job, then there were authorities who were responsible for changing that.

She didn't like what was happening in and around town, but this wasn't her fight. For now, and hopefully a long time, she was a book seller. A local trader. The corners of her lips flicked up. Trader. Sounded nice.

Charlotte turned onto the path to the falls. The sounds and smells of the bush surrounded her, and she breathed deeply of the fragrant air. It wasn't long before the familiar roar of the waterfall interwove with the birdsong. She stopped at the information board.

She'd not looked at it since the first night when she'd run in an emotional panic into the dark. The map of the area showed several walking tracks with expected time for the average person. One led a longer way, avoiding the lookout to climb to the top of the falls.

Perfect.

After a sip of water, Charlotte found the entry to the new track, a bit excited to see some new part of the falls. The walk, according to the board, was a one-hour round trip, so she'd be back home before dark, even with a stop for photos.

Whoever came up with one-hour timeframe must have been a power-walker. The track was even worse than the ramp past the lookout. At times, Charlotte had to grab branches to support herself as she clambered up spots where steps had completely rotted. Coming back would be interesting.

The track did a long, slow curve and then abruptly stopped at the bottom of a high flight of steps. As in, so high Charlotte could barely see the top. Her stomach rumbled. Keep going or turn back and find somewhere to sit for while? She didn't recall anything other than dense undergrowth and trees on either side of the path, so sucked on the water bottle again and began the ascent.

Halfway up, she seriously reconsidered the decision. These steps were steep and deep, requiring more than normal work. Her calf and thigh muscles screamed at her.

Think how strong you'll get if you did this more often.

If she survived.

One last push and she was at the top, breathing fast and feeling just a little lightheaded. The roaring in her ears died down and she blinked to clear her vision. Except, the roaring wasn't just from her elevated heartbeat. Up here, the falls were loud as a river rushed to the edge of the cliff and threw itself over.

The view was spectacular. From here, the peaks of the hills around the town surrounded her. In the distance was a mountain. Mt Macedon, she assumed, from the shape and direction. And below was the pool with its surrounding meadow of green and a narrowing river that would eventually become little more than a wide creek that wound past the township.

Charlotte moved closer to the river and found a place to sit beneath a tree. There, she ate her sandwich as clear water rushed by on its descent to the next phase of its life.

A bit like me.

From one place to another. Always Charlie but changing a little each time. She enjoyed the analogy. The river had no concept of its approach to the falls yet flowed with purpose and courage. No deviations or sudden stalls in case something ahead might be scary.

She took some selfies with the river in the background. These would go onto her screensaver as a reminder of the power of nature and the value of its lessons.

Phone in her hand, Charlotte climbed over a few rocks to reach the edge of the cliff. The late afternoon sun still stung, in fact, it was hotter now than earlier in the day. Distant clouds were dark and thick and heading this way. She'd need to leave soon.

But first the scenery demanded her attention. She was just far enough away from the point the water cascaded to get some beautiful images. Then, there was the pool from this vantage point. It was clear to the bottom apart from the base of the falls which churned and clouded the water. Finally, back across the canopy to the lookout.

Someone was there.

She zoomed in.

Two someones. A young dark-haired man and older lady. Glenys. *How curious.*

The man carried a bunch of flowers which he handed to Glenys. She nodded to him, then held the flowers out over the rail. It was too far for Charlotte to see details, but when the flowers were released, Glenys covered her face. The man put a hand on her shoulder.

Rosie's voice crept into Charlotte's mind. Words about Glenys. "…her poor husband—God rest his poor soul…I hope nobody fell down the steps to the Falls again."

A chill crept up Charlotte's spine and she lowered the phone. Had Mr Lane fallen from the lookout? This might be a remembrance ritual for Glenys. She didn't want to intrude but needed just another quick look at the man she was with.

When she raised the phone and zoomed the camera in, it was straight into his face. He was no more than twenty-five, with a tattoo on his neck of some sort. And he was staring back at her as if he had eagle eyes.

"How?" She backtracked, slipping behind a taller rock. How did he know she was there? Or was this pure coincidence and he was gazing up at the top of the falls, waiting for Glenys to want to leave. It was such a long way she doubted if anyone could identify a person. But the chill remained.

After a moment, she took a careful peek around the rock. They were gone. If they were heading back to the road, she wouldn't come across them. She'd hate to interrupt what appeared to be a sad event for Glenys. And a part of her hoped she hadn't been seen.

CHAPTER THIRTY-FIVE

Even as Charlotte attempted to sweep the pavement outside the shop, customers wanted to go inside. She smiled, followed them in, and let them browse as she put the broom away. There'd be time later.

The heavy clouds from yesterday never made it to Kingfisher Falls but the day was less humid, and Charlotte hoped the nice weather would bring shoppers out in droves. So far, so good.

Rosie arrived as the first customers left, the frown on her face at odds with her cheerful Christmas hat. She wheeled straight around the counter and tapped on the computer.

"Good morning." Charlotte joined her. "Okay, since when do you have a Facebook account?" Rosie had refused Charlotte's offer to walk her through the setup the other day, preferring to avoid social media.

"One learns when one must."

"And why must you be on Facebook?"

The look Rosie gave her was serious. "When a neighbour tells me there are things I need to see on my bookshop's page. That's why."

"Oh." Charlotte sat.

"Oh, indeed." Rosie scrolled through the bad reviews, the frown deepening. "Why not tell me?"

"Because they are fake reviews."

"I don't understand. This one says we told a customer to leave."

"Exactly. May I?" Charlotte gently took the mouse. "Right. This one...see the name of the reviewer? It belongs to a made-up account. And I've reported it. And this. This. And look, another with almost the same name."

"Sid Browne. Backwards."

Charlotte's mouth opened in surprise.

"I play a lot of word games. I'm going to call him." She reached for the phone.

"No, no, don't. Please."

"Charlie, I am tired of this nonsense! And hurt. Ever since Christmas trees began disappearing, this shop seems to be under attack! Octavia, and Marguerite, even Glenys! And Sid's had it in for you from day one." Rosie's eyes glistened.

"Don't cry. And please don't call him. Not yet."

"Not yet?" Rosie drew in a long breath.

"I've also reported his own Facebook page so it is possible all of this will disappear soon. Rosie, I think we need some advice about how to handle Sid Browne, don't you?"

"A lawyer?"

Charlotte smiled. "Was thinking more of asking another police officer about the processes to make a complaint that will stick."

"Trevor."

"Can we shelve this until we see him?"

"I'll think about it." Rosie took off her glasses to dab her eyes. "Right. So, what did you get up to yesterday?"

Keeping an eye on the front door for customers, Charlotte gave Rosie an edited version of the previous day's events. Not wishing to upset her further, she left out her venture as an amateur sleuth following the ute, and where it ended up, as well as her suspicions about Veronica. Although she did ask about the woman's history of opening and closing shops.

"I'd forgotten about that. At first, we...you know, the older traders and I, thought she simply had no idea what she was doing. The existing shoe shop was appalled but tried to be friendly. It was Veronica's rudeness from the beginning which surprised us all."

"What about the homewares?"

"Dear Lewis was beside himself. He's owned his shop for decades and was always a fair trader. Looks out for other people. Veronica moved in over a long weekend when his shop was closed, and he arrived the following Tuesday to find her A-frame signage blocking his front door. Anyway, customers worked her out quickly and she was packed up and gone within weeks."

"Does she have family? I heard her say she's a single mother."

"Of two adult daughters who left home before she moved here. When did you meet Lewis?" Rosie clicked out of Facebook and back to the sales screen.

"Yesterday. He mentioned a Christmas Eve party."

"Yes. I told you all about…oh. I didn't. Did I?"

"Was it my blank expression that gave it away?" Charlotte grinned. "Are you going to it?"

"Always. And so should you."

"Just as well I went shopping this morning and stocked up. What should I bring?"

———

The morning was so busy that Rosie didn't stop smiling. Charlotte's legs ached with every step and she blamed the steep steps to the waterfall for that. But the atmosphere of joyful buying and cheery customers was enough to make her forget her tiredness.

People dropped in gifts for Rosie. By lunchtime she had a shopping bag full of them behind the counter.

"I'm thinking of running this home. That way I won't have too much to carry tonight if more come." Rosie put a hand over her mouth. "Oh, listen to me, almost expecting gifts!"

The first chance she got, she hurried out. Charlotte longed to sink onto her stool for a short break, but the shelves weren't going to tidy or restock themselves, so she sipped some water and got back to work.

She carried an armful of books from the storeroom to replace recently sold titles. Halfway into the shop, the hair stood up on the back of her neck and she looked around. Nobody was there.

"Rosie?"

No answer. And she'd have heard the buzzer. Something made her look out of the window. The blue ute was parked across the street. A man leaned back on the bonnet, his legs and arms crossed as he stared straight at her. The man from the lookout.

Charlotte couldn't move. Or breathe. He had seen her yesterday and more than that, he knew her. The books grew heavy in her arms. She was going to drop them unless she put them down.

Move, legs.

She forced herself to the counter, the books spilling onto it as her arms gave way. After righting the pile, she looked outside.

He wasn't at the ute.

Was he coming in here?

The phone was in her hand in an instant but then the familiar sound of the ute's motor made her pause. It U-turned slowly, the passenger window wound right down. As he passed, the man gave her the finger.

Charming.

Bit by bit, Charlotte's heartbeat returned to normal and her legs co-operated. Anger kicked the fear to the kerb. He could stare into the shop with a mask, or directly at her without one, but now she knew his face, he was in her sights.

———

Her bold thoughts settled to more moderate and sensible ones by the time Rosie returned. She needed to talk to Trev, but away from Rosie. Whatever that young man, and Sid, and a few of the others in town had going on required careful consideration, not rushing in and taking risks with nothing but hunches and a few photos that didn't match up.

"You look deep in thought, darling. Were you rushed off your feet?"

"Busy for almost the whole time. Oh, is that an iced chocolate for me?" Charlotte almost clapped her hands as Rosie placed the cup holder on the counter.

"It is. The caffeine will help."

"Yummy, thank you." After a long sip through the straw, Charlotte sighed. "I needed this so much."

"You deserve it. And you've even restocked and tidied. Nobody should ever complain about how this little shop looks."

"Speaking of people who complain..." Charlotte finally sat on her stool and stretched her legs. "Glenys."

"Was she in again?"

"No. But yesterday when I was at the top of the falls, I noticed her at the lookout. She had flowers."

Rosie nodded. "Of course. It would be to remember her poor husband. Must be around fifteen years ago he slipped off that very place."

"I assumed as much. What a dreadful thing. She had someone with her."

"One of the ladies?" Rosie said.

"A young man. Dark, longish hair. Twenties."

"Hm. Doesn't sound familiar. Perhaps her nephew. Her brother used to live in town and was a bit of a hell-raiser. Ended up in prison and his family moved. Never been back. But there was a son."

Oh, Glenys. Are you harbouring a criminal?

CHAPTER THIRTY-SIX

WHATEVER GLENYS MIGHT BE UP TO, CHARLOTTE HAD NO MORE time to worry about it, or the rather rude young driver of the blue ute. The remainder of the day flew by and before she knew it, Rosie was waving the final customer goodbye and closing the front door.

"Already?"

"You, my darling, are a natural retailer. What you've done this past week or two is nothing short of amazing and I am proud of you!" Rosie reached her hand out and when Charlotte took it, pulled her down to kiss her cheek. "Very proud."

Charlotte couldn't stop smiling as a lovely warmth filled her heart. She'd rarely been praised in her life and no longer expected it, so these words from the lady she respected so much meant the world.

Rosie pulled the metal cash box out from beneath the counter. "Are you happy for me to donate all the notes to Darcy's family?"

"I can think of no better recipient. How will we get it to them, and the books? Shall I drive up tonight?"

"No need. I spoke to Abbie earlier and they are bringing Lachie down for the Christmas Eve party. One of the local grandfathers always dresses as Santa and I'm going to get him to make sure the money is put directly into Darcy's hands. Not that anyone other than you and I know what will be inside a gift-wrapped box with his name on."

"So, shall I wrap?"

"Yes please. I saved that little box back there and will go get the rest of the money." Rosie disappeared to the back. Charlotte put all the books for Lachie into a bigger box, then selected plain brown wrapping paper. This was her favourite, because then she could add some colourful ribbons and a bow and know it was fully recyclable.

"What time is this party?" Charlotte called as she finished wrapping.

"In an hour. Gives people a chance to get home from work and freshen up. I might go and do that myself, if you're fine to close the registers?" Rosie returned to the counter with the remaining wad of cash. "I'm so happy. Do you know, the generous people of this town helped us raise almost five hundred dollars? I just put the last twenty in to round it up."

"Oh, Rosie that's wonderful! That much money might give the Forests a little bit of breathing space."

"All thanks to your ideas." Rosie collected her handbag and another full bag of gifts. "My goodness, I'm keeping fit just by lugging this around, but aren't I spoilt?"

Yes, she was, and rightly so. Charlotte let Rosie out through the front door and locked it behind her, turning the open sign to closed. She was loved, respected, and admired in Kingfisher Falls.

Which made it all the stranger that people like the book club ladies were suddenly turning their backs. Charlotte hurried up. She wasn't going to dwell on the idiosyncrasies of the few. Not when there was a Christmas party to attend.

———

A shower later, Charlotte stared at her open wardrobe. The only parties she'd attended in her life were workplace ones. This one was an outdoor, casual event, but she didn't want to wear shorts and T-shirt. She held a dress in front of herself. Better to keep for dinner tomorrow. There was a tropical looking blouse she'd picked up somewhere, so she teamed it with a skirt and put sandals on her bare feet.

When she'd shopped before work this morning, she'd agonised over what to take tonight. Lewis had said everyone took a plate, and Rosie wasn't even worried about her taking anything, but she was going to. She'd settled on a pile of cute gingerbread cookies, all in different shapes. Admittedly, they were from the bakery department of the supermarket, but baked in-house. One day she'd learn to do all of this herself.

With an apologetic glance at the gingerbread house kit pushed to the back of the counter, Charlotte covered the box of cookies with foil and threw her handbag over her shoulder.

Nerves almost got the better of her. She stared at the door, box in her hand, and bit her lip a bit harder than expected. This was her new home. Kingfisher Falls. And most of the people were amazing, she knew this from meeting so many customers. Plus, Esther and Doug, Lewis, and the lovely people at both restaurants.

Stop overthinking, Charlie.

But what if Sid was there? And the book club ladies? Or Veronica and the councillors and even worse, the blue ute boys, as she'd begun to think of them.

Charlotte walked out onto the balcony and looked down the street. Cars were pulling up along the kerbs on both sides, families wandered toward the plaza, and as the light slowly faded, the beautiful Christmas lights began to dance. Music drifted over.

Her little tree sparkled in the last of the sunlight.

"Tell me what to do." She whispered. "Go, or stay here and hide?"

Even as she spoke, she grinned. "Guess I'll be partying, huh?"

———

Down on the street, she almost changed her mind seeing Sid and Marguerite, arm in arm as they strolled ahead. It was a first to see him in anything other than a police uniform or his more standard attire of tracksuit pants and singlet. Tonight, he wore a bright

Hawaiian shirt and shorts. His legs were even hairier than his shoulders.

"Bother." She glanced at her own top, but at least hers didn't have giant pineapples all over it.

The plaza was alive with movement and sound. Past the fountain, trestle tables lined up to form a long, narrow table filled with all manner of goodies. A giant seafood platter took pride of place on one table. Further along was a huge Christmas cake. In between was everything from salads, to cheese platters, and lots of turkey and ham.

Charlotte found an empty corner and sliding her box onto the table, took the foil off.

"Store bought! We make our own delicacies." Octavia's voice carried from three tables away.

Marguerite was with her, looking at Charlotte like something a cat dragged in. Although if it was Mayhem, he was more likely to take down Marguerite and spit her out. Charlotte giggled.

Octavia pursed her lips and Marguerite patted her arm. "I'm sure she's been drinking, love. Who'd laugh at being told they don't fit in and never will?"

"I think you are right." Octavia picked up a skewer of some kind and it promptly spilled sauce all over her white dress. "Oh my God!"

Before she burst into laughter, Charlotte turned away. She should have offered a napkin but wasn't in the mood. Darcy, Abbie, and Lachie stood back from the tables, their aloneness obvious. Lachie was wide-eyed at the laden tables, and then he spoke to his dad and a moment later, headed for the fountain.

"Hello!" Charlotte waved as she approached. Darcy and Abbie held hands. "Thank goodness you are here. I'm a bit nervous about all of this."

"You are?" Abbie's face was drawn. "But you live here."

"I'm the newbie. And I'm shy by nature."

"No need, Charlie." Darcy grinned the way he did the first time they met. "Lots of friendly folk around."

"Not all friendly." Abbie's voice was quiet. Darcy nudged her gently with his shoulder. "Would you like something to eat?"

"We didn't bring anything."

"Hah!" Charlotte said. "Then you're perfect for the yummy gingerbreads that I've just been told off about. Store bought at the last minute."

Something like a smile flickered on Abbie's face. "I'm still getting used to small towns. In the city we'd never do anything like this."

"Then go and enjoy."

"Babe, I might find something." Abbie kissed Darcy's cheek and wandered to the closest table.

"I really am happy you are here." Charlotte turned to Darcy. "You may not know, but the bookshop had a giving box this year, and lots of people donated books with different age groups, genres, interests and the like."

His smile disappeared.

Oh, Darcy. Don't expect the worst.

"Do you know how many people asked if they could give a book to Lachie? And before you go all proud and protective on me, you need to know why. Okay?"

Lips pressed together, Darcy nodded.

"Cool. That kid of yours makes people happy. His manners and willingness to help out is not unnoticed. And the fact he calls Abbie 'Mrs Forest' is kinda cute. You need to admit that." Charlotte grinned at Darcy and at last, his face softened into a sort-of-smile.

"So," she continued. "There's a box of books for him for Christmas. All appropriate, and all very well wrapped I might add."

"Your work?"

"Darcy, I can only imagine how much you've had to contend with. You and your family are amazing people. Please don't reject a little bit of help at this time of year, when so many people want to feel good about giving."

Lachie ran over and grabbed his father's leg. "Dad, daddy. Santa's gonna be here!"

"Is that right?" Darcy said. "Have you said hello to Charlotte?"

"Hello, Charlotte. Is your tree quite well?"

Charlotte almost collapsed in laughter at the adult tone coming from a child's mouth, but she kept her face serious. "The tree is very well. It thanks you for asking."

The look he gave her almost broke her resolve.

"Trees do not speak. Perhaps we should check this tree in case it has become an alien."

"Oh. You like aliens?"

"He loves aliens." Abbie returned with a small plate of food. "The scarier, the better."

"Santa is an alien!" Lachie announced, over his shoulder as he ran back toward the fountain.

"This is true." Charlotte observed.

"Sorry about yesterday." Darcy looked at the ground. "Got some bad news and it felt like the final straw."

Abbie leaned her head on his shoulder and his arm went around her. A little twinge of wistfulness touched Charlotte. Time to move along. "My advice is get a big plate of Christmas fare before Sid and the book club ladies consume the lot. That's where I'm off to now."

CHAPTER THIRTY-SEVEN

SHE DIDN'T GET AS FAR AS THE TABLES. ROSIE WHEELED TOWARD her, waving in an urgent fashion that had Charlotte weaving through people to reach her near the fountain.

"There's been another..." Rosie lowered her voice, glancing around. "Another break-in. Another tree gone. My neighbour. Arrived home from work ready to begin preparing for tomorrow's lunch with their relatives and the back door was wide open."

Rosie stopped to draw breath and Charlotte squeezed her arm, squatting at her side to keep the conversation private. A few people glanced their way. "And the tree was gone?"

"Yes. Tree, and this time something else was taken. They're expecting their first grandchild and had a highchair set up ready to give them."

"Oh, no."

"Oh, yes. So specific." Rosie gazed at the Forests, who were sitting on a bench a little distance away with plates.

"Rosie! They didn't do it."

"I know. But someone wants to make it look that way."

Surely nobody would accuse the family of stealing a highchair. What was next? Charlotte got to her feet as Glenys appeared through the partygoers, looking around until she saw Octavia and Marguerite. In a moment they were huddling around Glenys' phone.

"What's she showing them?" Rosie was at a disadvantage from her position. "Is it on a phone?"

"Yes. And they're getting all riled up. Rosie, we might need to—"

Rosie was already on her way to the Forests to get there before the book club ladies. They, led by Octavia, ploughed through anyone who was in their way without so much as an 'excuse me'. This couldn't end well. Charlotte chased after Rosie.

At the bench, Darcy was on his feet, in front of Abbie and Lachie as though protecting them. Abbie clutched Lachie to her, hands over his ears as Octavia bellowed at them.

"—of all the sneaky, underhand and cruel things to do!"

"Stop it!" Rosie got there just before Charlotte. "Octavia, lower your voice before you frighten the child."

"The child? Who cares about the baby who now won't have a highchair!" Octavia's face was bright red and her hands in fists against her hips. "What do you have to say for yourself, Darcy Forest? What excuse do you have?"

The music stopped. People turned to watch. Some moved closer. For an instant, the only sound was the gurgling of the fountain.

Darcy took a step forward. "I have no idea what you are yelling about, Mrs Morris. None."

"Liar." That was Marguerite.

Where was Sid? Charlotte couldn't see him amongst the crowd.

"Ladies, please. This is a Christmas party. Not the Spanish Inquisition." Rosie spun her chair, so she was at Darcy's side, facing the three women. "What is the problem?"

"None of your business, Rosie Sibbritt." Marguerite snarled.

Rosie blinked a few times, but her voice was steady and calm. "You've made this everyone's business. I think you owe us all an explanation."

Onlookers formed a circle around the bench, obviously agreeing.

Glenys tapped on her phone and then showed an image to Darcy. "This." Then swiped. "And this." She held the phone higher and showed it to the crowd.

The photos were in a pine forest clearing. The first was of a pile of broken artificial trees. The second was a wider shot and included a tipped over highchair with a bow around it.

People strained to see. "Where is it?" and "Is that a highchair?" rustling through the crowd like leaves in the wind.

"I'll tell you." Glenys put the phone away, addressing the group of onlookers but avoiding Darcy's confused gaze. "That clearing is next door to my property. Darcy Forest has been working along the fence for a while which I thought was a good thing, getting rid of undergrowth at this time of year. Until I happened to find those! All the stolen Christmas trees and a highchair."

"And I heard someone stole a brand-new highchair today which was ready to be given to new parents." Marguerite's tone of voice was triumphant. "I wonder who else is having a baby!" She pointed at Abbie. "Oh look. You wouldn't be in need of some baby items now, would —"

"Stop it!" Darcy grabbed Abbie's hand and helped her to her feet. Tears streamed down her face and Lachie clung to her, his face white and eyes wide. "Leave us alone. We've done nothing wrong. Nothing." He led his family away, the crowd parting as he walked.

An uncomfortable silence fell. Some people wandered away, while others waited for the book club ladies to say something more. Rosie cleared her throat and eyes turned to her.

"Marguerite, you should be ashamed." Her words were delivered in a calm monotone, as though having a pleasant chat about nothing in particular. "That little family needs our love, not your vitriol. Darcy is no thief."

Octavia turned on Rosie. "Believe whatever fantasies you want. He obviously cut up the big tree in the roundabout with his chainsaw and has been hiding the evidence. I told you they are bad, those Forests. Every last one of them."

"Are you saying little Lachie is a bad person?" Doug appeared, Esther at his side.

"Oh, no, Lachie is a lovely little boy. Octavia didn't mean that." Glenys finally spoke again. She'd paled over the past few minutes and leaned heavily on her walking stick. "But it's so odd all those trees and the highchair are there on the Christmas Tree farm. Isn't it?"

Charlotte's heart raced. All this anger and finger-pointing felt personal. Someone could do their best and still be blamed for something outside their control. She played with the bracelet, stretching it and letting it snap back to remind herself…don't get involved. This wasn't her fight. But she knew Darcy wasn't the thief. His chainsaw might be the one used to destroy the big tree, but she'd been there just after he'd discovered it dumped on the opposite side of his property.

Do something, Charlie. Say what you know.

Voices were rising as Octavia and Marguerite argued with Doug and Rosie. Charlotte slipped away through a gap in the crowd. Her fingers worked the bracelet, round and round, then snap and snap. She had to find a quiet place to think.

At the corner of the plaza she paused and glanced back. The long trestle tables with their Christmas fare were almost unattended. All the action was around the bench where the Forest family had been minding their own business. How distressing for Abbie, and poor Lachie. Even under such fire, Darcy kept his cool. If only they'd stayed a little longer to hear Rosie and Doug stand up for them.

Charlotte headed for the alley that would lead toward the bookshop. A few moments to work through this and she'd go back. Make sure Rosie was okay. See what could be done to make it up to the Forests.

Just before she turned into it, there was another raised voice. This came from the alley and if she wasn't mistaken, it belonged to Veronica.

CHAPTER THIRTY-EIGHT

CHARLOTTE CREPT TO THE CORNER AND PEEPED AROUND. Veronica stood, hands on hips, in the middle of the alley. She screeched at someone just out of sight. The words made no sense.

"...made me look bad. Made me look like I'm behind this mess of yours!"

Now who upset her?

A muffled male voice answered. Too quiet for Charlotte to hear. Dared she go closer? Between here and Veronica was a row of skip bins, large receptacles for recycling and some for garbage. If Charlotte was careful, she could slip between them and the wall of the alley.

If she sees you...keep walking. Don't do it.

Charlotte slid behind the first bin and stopped, holding her breath.

"And it isn't fair!" The screeching reduced to a loud whine. "I really, really like you."

"Me too, darl. You're fun."

"Then why won't you come to the plaza with me?"

There was no answer and Charlotte was forced to find a gap between bins to see through. Veronica was being kissed by the man

180

from yesterday. So, was this simply a lover's quarrel? But what had Veronica meant by her 'looking bad'?

After a couple of kisses, Veronica pushed him away, not angrily, but like a petulant child. "Don't try to get on my good side. Either you're coming with me and I can give you a decent alibi, or —"

"What, darl? You gonna tell tales on me?" He stepped toward Veronica. "Not like you're such a good girl."

"Get stuffed, Hank. I don't tell tales but I'm planning on partying." She spun away and tip-tapped on her high heels in Charlotte's direction. Fury reddened her face and with her chin high she wasn't looking for eavesdroppers. A moment later, the tip-tap faded, and she was gone.

Hank was on his phone, not looking the least bit concerned she'd left although he stared after her. Charlotte kept still. She wanted to hear him, and she didn't want to be seen.

Why do you get yourself into these things?

"I got rid of her." He spoke to the phone. "Not like that, you idiot. She's gone to the street party so come and get me if you still want to knock over your aunt's place." Hank listened. "Fine, Darro. I'll make sure the old bag is still at that stupid party."

He jogged past Charlotte.

Glenys had been tricked into making everyone believe Darcy was the thief. And with him gone from the street party, would he be blamed for a robbery at the house next door? The house owned by his accuser.

Charlotte stretched the bracelet.

Then took it off and tossed it into one of the bins.

———

Hank moved quickly, crossing the road with barely a look for traffic, before heading for the plaza. Charlotte sprinted to keep him in sight. If he saw her, she was in trouble. But if she lost him, Darcy was.

Charlotte's mind raced. How was she going to stop this from happening. She could hardly follow the ute to Glenys' property. Or she could find Sid.

Great options. Not.

She'd have to wing it. Call the emergency police number if it came to that.

He'd vanished. Charlotte stopped at the edge of the plaza. There was music playing again and she was relieved the crowd had dissipated and people were back around the tables.

Veronica was involved in an animated conversation with Jonas near the fountain. There was no sign of Rosie, Doug, or Esther. The book shop ladies were at the far end of a table, filling plates.

"Why are you following me?"

Charlotte froze.

"Do you think I didn't know?" Hank was right behind her.

"Why would I follow you? You're the one wearing masks at night and stealing Christmas trees. Aren't you?"

Veronica had her hands on her hips, glaring across the distance at Charlotte.

"I guess this was all your girlfriend's idea?" Charlotte said.

Hank stepped in front of her, his bulk blocking her sight of the other people. A sense of isolation swept through her.

"Guess again." He snarled.

"Oh. Sorry. Darro's idea? Couldn't be yours."

"You got a smart mouth for someone in danger. Really big danger."

"Scary."

Hank moved closer. He smelt almost as bad as Sid.

"See, I'm cool with tough guys." Charlotte nodded. "I am. One tied me up in a cave once. He's in prison now. Almost blew his hand off with a gun. Him, not me." She smiled. "I wouldn't have missed."

His hands snaked up to grasp her neck.

"Let me go."

"You think you know what's going on in this town. You need to mind your own business."

Charlotte's heart pounded as his fingers tightened. Her hands pushed against his chest until he laughed.

"Not so cocky now." Hank forced her backwards.

She had no strength to stop him. Step by step they were moving away from the party. From people. From help. He was going to kill her. Charlotte stopped pushing against him and reached for his face, seeking his eyes.

"Bitch. Don't."

"Help me!" Her cry came out as a whimper as he squeezed her windpipe. Her feet reached the edge of the footpath.

"You just had to interfere. Reporting us to the police. Watching us dismantle the tree in the roundabout from the shadows."

A car was coming, she could hear it. She gripped his shirt to avoid being pushed into its path.

"I'm gonna bury you in the pine forest and add one more crime to Darcy Forest's list. And then I'm taking all the pretty things and cash from the old bag's house and Darro and me? We're gonna have the best party ever."

"You pathetic little boy!"

Thwack.

Hank's face contorted and he released Charlotte.

Mrs Lane?

"You planned to steal from me?"

Thwack.

Hank staggered to one side, but Charlotte refused to let go of his shirt as she gasped for air. As he straightened, she dragged him toward herself with every bit of strength and kneed him in the crotch.

He screamed and collapsed to the ground, writhing around.

"I did tell you to let go." She managed.

Glenys stood over him, her walking cane raised and her face purple with fury. "Why? Why would you and my nephew hurt this town and hurt me?"

Hank was in no condition to answer. Charlotte put an arm around Glenys' shoulder.

———

"Darling, what on earth were you thinking?" Rosie refused to let go of Charlotte's hand. "He hurt you."

"Rosie, did you see how he hobbled away clutching his crotch?" It made Charlotte boil that despite her well-placed knee and Glenys' whacks with her cane, Hank still got away. In the panic from milling partygoers, he'd managed to drag himself off and straight into the blue ute which screeched to the kerb a minute after he went down.

Veronica had reached them surprisingly fast in her heels, with Jonas just behind, dialling his phone as he ran. She screamed at Charlotte to move and tried to throw herself on Hank, who at that point was still squealing. He'd pushed her away, and Jonas got between them.

"Oh, for goodness sake, people, don't let him go." Charlotte gave up and went to find Rosie. She was sitting outside Italia with Doug, Esther, and Lewis. Her arrival caused some fuss and it was a few minutes before she'd explained enough to make any sense to them. Doug took off, phone in hand. Charlotte's legs were shaky suddenly and she dropped onto a spare chair.

Sirens cut through the air but not past the plaza, so whether it was Sid or something else going on, Charlotte couldn't tell.

"I'm so sorry you were at risk, Charlie. Is your neck really okay?"

"Don't worry about me, Rosie. We need to let someone know." Charlotte sipped on a glass of water Lewis had rushed to get. "And somebody needs to check on Glenys."

"Someone has." Esther nodded toward the tables where Glenys was sobbing against Marguerite. Octavia, although patting Glenys' back, glared at Charlotte. "And...well, I don't think you have a friend there."

"Sorry, Rosie. I might have damaged the relationship with the book club."

"Don't start me on them! You are important. And after all of their little attempts to harm the shop...they can just go and—"

"Rosie Sibbritt!" Charlotte grinned. "I'm going to talk to your son about you."

"Go right ahead! He'll pat me on the shoulder and smile the way he does when there is nothing to say."

True. Charlotte was familiar with Trev's quiet ways. But he

wouldn't be happy Charlotte had been at risk. "I wish he hadn't escaped."

"You did well, darling. I'm just sorry you had to go through that. We were over here because I was so angry with Octavia and Marguerite that it seemed best to retreat and calm down. How dare they be so rude to the Forests?"

Lewis, who'd sat quiet through most of the conversations of the past few minutes, leaned forward, addressing Rosie with a steady tone. "They are wrong. And we need to come up with a way—as a town—to make it up to the family. Show them they are wanted here."

Yes. Yes, we do.

Charlotte stood. "I know what we should do."

All eyes turned to her.

"We need to pack this party up and take it to the Christmas Tree farm."

CHAPTER THIRTY-NINE

SOMEHOW, IT DIDN'T SURPRISE CHARLOTTE THAT LEWIS OWNED A minibus. The minute Rosie, Doug, and Esther agreed they'd get others involved in going to the Forests, he hurried off to collect it.

"Before his darling wife passed away, she ran the shop and he drove tourists around the area. To the wineries and Hanging Rock and all the other sights." Rosie puffed as she wheeled fast back to the other side of the fountain, Charlotte jogging to stay beside her. "I had no idea he still has the old thing so let's hope it's still driveable."

Doug and Esther were rounding people up, sending them to the fountain, and when there was a small crowd, Rosie parked herself in the middle.

"Sorry to interrupt your night yet again! We've had quite an evening. Terrible accusations and poor Charlotte threatened by a man who admitted to being one of the real Christmas tree thieves." Rosie's voice was calm and clear.

At the very outside of the circle, Marguerite and Octavia glowered at Charlotte. Glenys was nowhere to be seen and if she now knew her own nephew was behind the mayhem, she might have left to go home.

Would she be alright though? Doug had phoned Sid, who'd gone home early for a few drinks and complained about his evening being interrupted.

"A few of us are going to go to the Christmas Tree farm, and we'd like to invite you all."

"Now?" Someone called from the back. "What about the food?"

Charlotte stepped forward. "What if we take some of it up there. Enough for whoever comes along. We can set up in their carpark and ask them to join us."

"What a dreadful idea." Octavia was furious. "Those people are thieves."

"No, Octavia. No, they are not." Glenys hobbled her way to Rosie and Charlotte. Her face was puffy from crying, but she held her head high. "I am so sorry for my part in the whole mess. It would appear my nephew and his friend are responsible for stealing the trees and the probably the highchair."

"What about Santa though?" Another person from the back. "He'll be here soon and not everyone will want to traipse up to the farm tonight."

He'll cope. He's an alien.

"I believe Santa is pretty good at being in multiple places. Perhaps he would be kind enough to attend to both parties." Charlotte suggested, making eye contact with Esther, who was close friends with the gentleman taking on the role. She nodded and got her phone out.

"Right, so if nobody objects to us taking a table and some of the Christmas fare—"

"We object!"

Almost everyone in the crowd turned to Octavia and Marguerite. Nobody said a word, just stared. Marguerite grabbed Octavia's arm.

"We're leaving. And we're taking our food with us."

When there was no move to stop them, they stalked to the tables and began piling plates up to carry away.

The crowd thinned. Veronica, Jonas, and now Terrance were at the far edge of the plaza. Not talking. Just watching. There was something going on with them. Something more than Veronica's shock about her boyfriend, or the councillors' possible shady dealings. Unease settled in Charlotte's stomach. They were up to no good and this vendetta of the book club ladies wasn't the only strange behaviour in Kingfisher Falls.

———

The minibus nosed slowly into the driveway at the Christmas Tree Farm, Lewis careful of potholes and the odd kangaroo crossing the way in the dark.

Rosie was in the front passenger seat, lifted in by Doug, who then closed and packed her wheelchair. All twenty seats were full, and several cars followed, including Glenys', who'd said she wanted to apologise to Darcy. Once Lewis had arrived at the plaza it took only minutes to pack up some tables and lots of goodies. Santa had promised Esther to head up there after his plaza duties.

"I hope this won't make things worse." Charlotte was next to Esther. "What if Darcy and his family are so upset, they tell us to leave?"

Esther smiled. "It will be fine, you'll see. The books for Lachie are packed in the back as well as the baby hamper."

"The what?"

"Didn't Rosie tell you? She spent Sunday collecting all sorts of baby gifts. Doug provided a dinner for two voucher for Italia for when they're ready, and I'll babysit that night. And I've added a gift voucher so Abbie can choose some new clothes once she has her body back."

Tears prickled at the back of Charlotte's eyes. Tonight, after all the upsets and fears, this little town reminded her of River's End at its finest. She stared out the window, blinking to clear any mistiness.

Through the trees was a light. Then another. On and off. Someone walking through the pine trees. Charlotte thought it was still on Darcy's land, but couldn't be sure. He might be out checking his boundary. Or perhaps it was Sid. But it wouldn't hurt to be sure.

CHAPTER FORTY

THE CARPARK WAS DARK AND DESERTED. THERE WERE NO LIGHTS around the sheds, but the back of Abbie's car was visible near the house and a few rooms were lit.

After Lewis parked, Doug settled Rosie back in her chair. "I'm going to find Darcy and invite the family to our party." She said. "Do you want to come with me?"

"Actually, if you are okay on your own, I might help here."

"I know the way. See you soon, Charlie."

Charlotte stepped away from the minibus, scanning the trees. Nothing. If anyone had been out there, they'd gone.

As cars joined the minibus, people began unpacking tables. Everyone was occupied. Charlotte took her phone out and found the flashlight app, not turning it on just yet. Not unless she needed to.

She reached the trees at the edge of the carpark and walked a short way in. Still no lights or signs of anyone. About to turn back, a noise drifted through the pines. A motor running.

I'll look. That's all. Just look.

Flashlight on, Charlotte wound through the trees, avoiding branches and watching her step. She wanted to be quiet.

The motor was louder and now there was some light. Headlights.

She glanced back but the carpark was out of her sight. Charlotte turned her flashlight off and inched forward. Two figures crossed back and forth between her and the headlights, dragging what looked like branches.

There was a wire fence. Charlotte stopped at the edge of a small clearing between the trees and fence. On the other side, the blue ute idled. Darro and Hank were tossing all the evidence over the fence. The broken parts of synthetic Christmas trees, and then the highchair, one of its legs breaking as it hit the ground.

"Hold it right there!"

Sid?

Darro and Hank froze, then burst into laughter. Hank picked up branches and threw them into the back of the ute.

"Hands behind your heads. I told you to hold it." Sid's shadow approached.

Charlotte struggled to see with the headlights in her direction, so she darted a few trees over. Sid stood near the front of the ute.

"Hey, Sid. Come to give us a hand, mate?" Darro leaned against the bonnet.

So, Sid was involved. Or complicit. Or just didn't care. Charlotte's heart sank. By the time she got back to the carpark for help, these three would be gone.

"You're an idiot, Darro. Just like your idiot father." Sid's hands moved fast and Darro was face down on the bonnet. "You think I'm gonna let you ruin everything?" In an instant, he had handcuffs on Darro.

Hank was backing away.

"Freeze, Hank. Freeze."

Sid raised his gun and Hank stopped, hands hovering in the air. But Darro slipped out of his grasp and sidled away in the other direction. Sid swung the gun from one to the other. "Dammit, you're both under arrest. Do I have to shoot you both?"

They kept moving, mocking Sid with sneers.

Charlotte closed her eyes for a moment, feeling for the bracelet. In the bin in the alley.

Rosie wouldn't be happy with her. Or Trev. She took a deep breath and opened her eyes.

"You shoot one, Senior Constable Morris, and I'll take out the other." Charlotte's voice rang out.

"What the hell?" Sid glanced her way, then back at Darro. "Last warning, idiot."

Hank had halted at Charlotte's voice and one hand covered his crotch.

Still hurts?

"Better get down on the ground, Hank. Got you in my sights and I already told you, I don't miss." She yelled in her toughest tone.

If this didn't work, she was going to have to run the fastest she'd ever run. And hope Sid didn't shoot her accidentally. Sid rolled his eyes. It wasn't going to work.

"Don't shoot!" Hank dropped to his knees.

"Dude, she's bluffing." Darro tried to run and Sid kicked his legs from under him.

"She's dangerous." Hank threw himself on the ground, face down.

The expression on Sid's face was priceless. If only she'd had her camera ready. It didn't last as he cuffed Hank and dragged him to Darro, kicking his legs again for good measure.

"Show yourself, doctor."

Damn. What does he think he knows?

Charlotte stepped into the clearing and waved. "Looks like you have everything under control, Sid. Good work."

"Get over here. Hand me your weapon."

"Can't. Sorry. Only made a verbal threat and that's a bit difficult to hand over. Anyway, got a party to attend."

She spun the other way and sprinted.

"Oi. Get back here."

As if.

"Merry Christmas!"

———

The carpark was quiet. Charlotte stopped at the edge of the trees, confused. The tables were full of Christmas fare, people stood around, and the minibus's headlights beamed light over the area and toward the house.

Rosie appeared out of the darkness from the house and then Darcy. He held Abbie's hand and she pulled back, so he stopped. Lachie grabbed his father's other hand.

The family gazed around as though not understanding what was happening in their carpark. Abbie shook her head.

Charlotte stepped out from the trees, ready to go to them. Tell them they were wanted and cared for and very welcome. But how could she speak for the town?

"Good tidings we bring, to you and your kin," Lewis sang loudly, perfectly, in a deep baritone, his arms outstretched to the Forests.

For a long moment, there was silence, then Rosie wheeled herself to Lewis. "Good tidings for Christmas and a Happy New Year!" The love in her voice reached across the distance to the family. Lachie jumped up and down, grinning.

Everyone sang. Charlotte sang, Doug and Esther, every person she saw. Except Abbie and Darcy. Their arms were wrapped tightly around each other in a hug and their shoulders shook. Abbie's head was on Darcy's shoulder and Lachie was patting them both in sympathy.

As the last notes of the chorus died down, Glenys planted herself halfway between the tables and the family.

"Please. I need to say something."

Lachie hid behind Darcy, who looked up, tears on his cheeks. Abbie raised her head, her face wet. All three were expecting the worst. Silence fell.

Glenys shifted her weight from one foot to the other, leaning heavily on her walking cane. "I must apologise, and I can only ask you to forgive me. Darcy, Abbie, and you, little Lachie, you've all been subjected to some awful accusations. Some of this is my fault. I believed what people said."

"What your friends did earlier was cruel, Glenys." Darcy spoke without malice, just with truth. "It hurt my family."

"I know. Tonight, I've discovered who the Christmas tree thief really is." She gulped, faltering. Her shoulders went back, and she found her voice. "My nephew has been staying with me with his friend. I don't know why they would, but I'm terribly sorry to say they were stealing from our town."

"Your nephew?" Abbie walked to Glenys. Darcy was close behind. "That's so awful for you. Are you alright?"

Glenys burst into tears and Abbie put an arm around her shoulders.

"See, knew they had nothing to do with it."

Charlotte hadn't seen Rosie approach and quickly wiped away some moisture that had strangely appeared on her own face. Even Rosie's eyes were suspiciously bright.

"You sing well." Charlotte said.

"Me? I'm in the local choir. So is Lewis. And wasn't that an inspired choice of song to show the Forests how much we love them?"

Inspired indeed. Rosie and Lewis are a good team.

"There's something I need to tell you, Rosie." Might as well get it over with and hope the Christmas spirit was going to keep Rosie from having a melt-down.

"Shall we get a drink and food while you tell me? I haven't had anything since lunch."

———

The opportunity passed as more carols were sung and people mingled, ate, and laughed. Darcy and Abbie were the happiest Charlotte had ever seen and even Glenys, although sad, sang along a couple of times. Lachie talked to everyone.

"Does your tree require my expertness to see if it's an alien?" he asked Charlotte. "If it is, we can call for help. But no returns."

"But I bought a tree. So, if it is an alien, I might want my money back."

"No returns, ma'am. That's the rules." He ran off to speak to Rosie.

"Charlie?" Abbie leaned a hand on a table, rubbing her back.

"Are you okay? Not going into labour?"

Abbie laughed. "Better not. January baby not a Christmas one. No, just tired and I'm going to bed soon." She took Charlotte's hand. "You're incredible. You made this happen."

"Hardly. Just made a suggestion."

"Uh huh. And worked out who the Christmas tree thief is. And gave us this beautiful evening. We've been struggling since we moved in." Her smile faded. "Darcy's father left things in a mess and with the town against us...well, we didn't know what to do."

"The town is behind you now. The three of you can do anything."

"Oh, what's happening now?" Abbie looked past Charlotte to the driveway.

Sid's patrol car, lights flashing, drove into the carpark and pulled up. Charlotte knew he'd come for her. After her antics in the trees, he probably believed she had a gun on her and was going to arrest her in front of everyone. Great timing.

He climbed out. Wearing a Christmas hat. There were a few giggles as he strutted around the door to the backseat.

"Aren't you lot missing someone?"

With a flourish he opened the door.

"Santa!" Lachie squealed and ran toward the man in the red suit.

"Merry Christmas!" Santa rang a bell as Sid dragged out a large sack from the seat. "Santa's here with some presents. Now, who's been nice?"

Santa was led to a stool that Lewis had grabbed from the minibus. Was there nothing he didn't have lying around? Sid carried the sack over and placed it on the ground, then headed back to the patrol car to turn off the lights.

Charlotte stood back. This was why Sid was here? Was there really a heart beating under all the rudeness and bravado?

"Don't imagine I've forgotten about you, missy."

She jumped. How had he snuck up on her?

"No idea why Hank was so scared of you. Helped, though."

"Have they told you why they did it?"

"Both insist they were hired anonymously and paid in cash left at an agreed point."

"There has to be more to it."

Sid scowled. "Not your problem."

"You're welcome."

He grunted. "I don't trust you, doctor."

Feeling's mutual.

Santa extracted the baby hamper from his sack and Abbie was again in tears. Darcy grinned at Charlotte and she shook her head with a smile, pointing to Rosie.

"You've done a good thing here, missy. But don't let it go to your head." Sid leaned closer and Charlotte wrinkled her nose. "Gonna find out exactly what made you come to my town. And what you left behind. Merry Christmas."

He headed to the table and began loading up a plate. Charlotte waited for the anxiety to rise. For the stone in her gut to make itself known. She touched her wrist. It would take a while to learn not to reach for the bracelet.

Lachie sat cross-legged on the ground near Santa, unwrapping a book. Rosie and Lewis chatted with Doug and Esther. People wandered around. Glenys and Sid were talking, and Charlotte's heart went out to her. But it was better to know. Somebody began singing 'Jingle Bells' and once again, the Christmas tree farm was alive with music and laughter. There was love here in this town.

Love and hope. Charlotte inhaled the heady scent of pine and night air. Love and hope.

CHAPTER FORTY-ONE

CHARLOTTE STARED INTO THE BOX IN THE SPARE ROOM. TO ONE side was a small collection of Christmas cards inside a plastic sleeve. Before she could change her mind, Charlotte grabbed them from the box and returned to the kitchen, where a half-finished cup of coffee cooled on the counter.

She'd slept so well last night. Yes, there were some concerns, mostly around Sid, but those paled against the incredible outpouring of support for the Forest family from so many people in the community.

Now mid-morning, Charlotte had a few hours before heading up to Rosie's place for dinner. Something led her to open that box again. She wasn't ready to go through the whole thing, but she wanted to look at these cards. The coffee was awful now, so she made another, then took it and the cards out on the balcony. The little tree sparkled as the sunshine lit up its ornaments.

"I can't return you, according to Lachie. Guess we're stuck with each other."

The tree swayed a little, obviously happy with its home.

One by one, Charlotte took the Christmas cards from their sleeve and made a small pile. She didn't remember any of them. There were nine in all. Each was a work of art as if created just for the recipient. And so individual. One was a white Christmas scene with a little town, another a beach Christmas. The card used was thick and of quality.

Why would her mother keep these, when she didn't do anything for Christmas? No presents or cards for her own family or anyone else. No dinner or decorations. No leaving stockings out for Santa. It wasn't that Angelica disliked Christmas, but as with every celebration she simply couldn't be bothered. Something about these cards meant something to her.

Charlotte opened the one on top. The handwriting was beautiful.

Merry Christmas, sweetie. You are loved. Z.

She frowned. 'Z' didn't tell her anything, and who was 'sweetie'? One by one she opened each card. The greeting was the same in each. Going through them again, she noticed a year written on the bottom right corner. After putting them in order, she read from oldest to newest.

Nothing was familiar. The years were those from her second to eleventh birthdays. Without envelopes or further details there was no way of knowing who the sender, or the recipient was. Most likely this was a friend of her mother's who'd now lost contact. Except, Charlotte could not remember her mother ever having a friend. Or even talking about a past friend. So, what was the story with these beautiful cards?

———

"It sounds as though your lunch was delicious, Mum." Charlotte listened to Angelica chatter about the Christmas Day lunch at Lakeview Care. Maggie had been thrilled to hear Charlotte's voice and promised to keep an eye on Angelica during their conversation, as she was prone to reacting badly to goodbyes.

"Best of all was having Daddy there."

Charlotte pulled her legs up under herself on the sofa. "Okay, Mum. That's nice."

Dad was so long gone it surprised Charlotte her mother remembered him. But sometimes Angelica's memory was razor sharp.

"Mum, can I ask a question?"

"Of course, but I'm not allowed to give away the recipe for the Christmas cake."

That made Charlotte smile. "Darn. I was hoping you could, but secrets are important to keep. I found some rather lovely Christmas cards but don't know who sent them."

"I have a Christmas card. It's from you."

"Yes, it is. I thought you'd like the kookaburra wearing the Christmas scarf."

"He's very cute."

"These are older cards, Mum. There's nine of them and they are really beautiful. Inside, each one says, 'Merry Christmas, sweetie —"

"You are loved. Z."

Charlotte's jaw dropped her mouth. That was one of her razor-sharp memory moments in action. "Wow wish I had such a great memory! So, who is 'Z'?"

Angelica laughed. "Stop teasing me. You know who."

"Must have forgotten. Can you remind me?"

There was a long silence. Charlotte knew she'd lost the moment. "Mummy?"

"I don't want to be here, Charlotte. Can you find Daddy and get him to pick me up. Now, please."

As her mother's voice rose, Charlotte heard Maggie in the background making soothing noises and then a minute later, she'd taken the phone from Angelica.

"Sorry, Doctor Dean, I think it might be time to take your mother for a nap."

"Thanks, Maggie. Tell her I love her and thank you for everything you do."

It was always the same now. Moments of clarity before the plunge back through time believing Charlotte was little and Dad was still there. Coupled with her other mental diseases and a lifetime of next to no treatments, Angelica's life had been empty of happiness.

"Not for you and not for me, Mum."

And unless Charlotte knew she wouldn't go down the same path, she wasn't about to bring another person into her life, only to destroy theirs.

———

"Those look delicious, darling. Thank you!" Rosie's smile lit the room, which was pretty enough already. The table was set outside and looked amazing. No food was out there yet, but candles nestled amongst flowers, and the setting of red and gold was so traditional Charlotte wanted to take a photo.

The delectable aromas from the kitchen made Charlotte's stomach rumble, and both cats sat on the back of the sofa staring into the kitchen. She set the salads down on the counter. "What can I do to help?"

"Pour us both a pre-dinner drink, if you will."

"Anything in particular?"

"You choose."

As Charlotte arranged drinks, Rosie went outside to check the table. "It looks wonderful." Charlotte brought her drink out. "To Christmas."

They clinked glasses and sipped.

"So, four places set?"

"Oh, one never knows who might need a meal. I always set an extra one." Rosie grinned, put her glass into the cup holder on her wheelchair, and went inside. "Wasn't last night wonderful? Apart from the dangerous stuff, but we will discuss that a little later."

Great.

"I think the Forests know they are welcome." Charlotte said.

"It certainly has shown a lot of people for who they truly are. I have to say, I am impressed by Glenys. Which reminds me. She phoned before to say Darren claims Veronica is involved. Trying to drum up her own tree sales."

"You don't believe him."

"It seems like a risky proposition just for a few sales." Rosie shook her head. "But this isn't our call. At least now there has to be an investigation."

"If Sid doesn't botch things." Charlotte sat on her usual chair and Mellow made a beeline for her lap just as there was a knock on the door. Rosie headed down the hallway and opened the door. "Oh, sweetheart, you made it!"

"Mum, you look wonderful."

He's here. This was a bad idea.

Charlotte made a big deal out of stroking Mellow's soft fur as footsteps approached. The last time she'd seen Trev was the day she left River's End to move here, so only a few weeks. Hardly any time. It wasn't as though they had anything going on. So why was her heartrate through the roof?

"Hey, Charlie."

And there he was, towering over Rosie in her wheelchair in T-shirt and jeans that as always showed off how fit he was. And his smile. And those eyes. Kind. And twinkling.

"Oh, Trevor. Hi."

Yeah, that sounded normal.

"Santa's Helper?" she said.

He touched his very Christmassy T-shirt. "Oh this? I had to take a very special gift to Thomas first, so this seemed appropriate."

"And you can tell us about it over dinner, but for now, throw your bag in your room and wash up. Charlie, like to help get the food out there? I think I heard Lewis pull up outside."

Charlotte shot a look at Trev, who'd frowned. But then warmth filled his eyes. "Sounds perfect, Mum."

In the kitchen, Rosie did a little wiggle in her chair. One might not know who needs a meal, but Rosie clearly had. Charlotte kept her smile hidden. She deserved happiness.

———

"All I did was pretend to have a gun from the safety of the trees. I was in no danger, and the bluff worked." Charlotte stabbed a piece of potato, all too aware of Trev's steady gaze on her. Rosie and Lewis had spent the last half hour filling Trev in on the recent events in the town. He'd said little. She wasn't about to look at him.

"Well, I think you are very brave, darling, but would prefer from now on that you do a little less detective work and stay safe." Rosie put her knife and fork on her plate with a satisfied sigh. "Who'd like some champagne?"

"I'll assist, if I may." Lewis stood and then followed Rosie to the kitchen.

"Charlie?"

Here we go.

"Trevor."

He reached his hand out and gently touched her neck. She knew there were finger-sized bruises and bit her lip.

"You did good."

Charlotte's eyes flew to his. That wasn't what she'd expected to hear.

His face was serious as he sat back. "I feel there's a whole lot of information missing, no doubt to stop Mum worrying even more, and I thank you for that."

"There's no point sharing every small detail."

"Except those are what add up to a bigger picture. Please take care. Don't let your guard down around Sid. Or Marguerite."

"Why? He's been hounding me since I got here. There's been comments about the past and you not having jurisdiction here. So, what happened?"

Rosie and Lewis shared a joke as they wandered back.

Trev shook his head. "Sid's just power hungry. Don't trust him."

Charlotte nodded.

"This is the loveliest Christmas dinner!" Rosie settled back at her place and Lewis poured glasses of champagne. "Thank you all for being here to celebrate with me."

They rose their glasses. Charlotte gazed around with an unfamiliar tightness in her chest. It might be happiness. Rosie, with her grace and kindness. Lewis, so sweet and caring. And Trev. His quiet confidence filled the room.

"To friends and family, near and far, to love and joy." Rosie made the toast. Mayhem jumped on her lap with a growl and everyone laughed.

At this moment, Charlotte understood what she'd always missed in her life. These wonderful people were what made Christmas real. No matter what might be ahead, she'd never forget her first real Christmas day.

"To Kingfisher Falls!"

EPILOGUE

THE LITTLE PINE TREE WAS PRETTY, EVEN WITHOUT ITS decorations. Charlotte put the last one into a small box and touched the top of the tree. "Thank you." She carried the box inside, then made coffee and returned to the balcony.

For the next week or so, the bookshop was closed, so Charlotte intended to spend time painting up here, exploring the back yard, and going through the storeroom in the garage. Something told her the contents of that room held all sorts of secrets.

Kingfisher Falls would return to its sleepy self, now that the Christmas tree thief—or thieves—were under lock and key, even if the mastermind was yet to be discovered.

Charlotte leaned against the railing and stared out over the town. So quiet now, the day after Christmas, but so much intrigue bubbling away beneath the surface.

A car slowly drove toward the bookshop from Rosie's end of town. Trev, going home to River's End. He was needed back there. Charlotte made eye contact through the windscreen and waved, and his arm flew out of the window to wave back. Then, he was gone. And a little bit of Charlotte went with him.

There'd been no more talk about Sid, but he was a danger to the town, perhaps to Rosie. If so, then he'd need to come through Charlotte. This was her home now, and no corrupt police officer or council, no vindictive book club ladies, or disgraced shop owners like Veronica would ever disrupt Kingfisher Falls again.

A breeze picked up, blowing Charlotte's hair about. She glanced the way Trev's car had gone. He'd be back, and when he did, she'd invite him on a picnic to the falls.

It was time to face the future without fear.

Dear reader,

We hope you enjoyed reading *Deadly Start*. Please take a moment to leave a review, even if it's a short one. Your opinion is important to us.

Discover more books by Phillipa Nefri Clark at https://www.nextchapter.pub/authors/phillipa-nefri-clark

Want to know when one of our books is free or discounted? Join the newsletter at http://eepurl.com/bqqB3H

Best regards,

Phillipa Nefri Clark and the Next Chapter Team

BOOKS BY PHILLIPA NEFRI CLARK

The Stationmaster's Cottage

Jasmine Sea

The Secrets of Palmerston House

The Christmas Key

Taming the Wind

Martha

Notes from the Cottage

Deadly Start

Deadly Falls

Deadly Secrets

Deadly Past

The Giving Tree

Colony

Table for Two

Wishing Well

Sculpture

Last Known Contact

Simple Words for Troubled Times (non-fiction)

Audiobooks

The Stationmaster's Cottage (bonus Taming the Wind)

Jasmine Sea (bonus Martha)

The Secrets of Palmerston House (bonus The Christmas Key)

Simple Words for Troubled Times

AUTHOR BIO

Phillipa lives just outside a beautiful town in country Victoria, Australia. She also lives in the many worlds of her imagination and stockpiles stories beside her laptop.

She writes from the heart about love, dreams, secrets, discovery, the sea, the world as she knows it... or wishes it could be. She loves happy endings, heart-pounding suspense, and characters who stay with the reader long after the final page.

With a passion for music, the ocean, animals, reading, and writing, she is often found in the vegetable garden pondering a new story.

Lightning Source UK Ltd.
Milton Keynes UK
UKHW010624160921
390678UK00001B/148